THE PYX

JOHN
Buell

THE PYX

HarperCollins*Publishers*Ltd

To my wife

This edition published by arrangement with
Farrar, Straus and Giroux, New York

Canadian Cataloguing in Publication Data

Buell, John, 1927-
    The pyx

ISBN 0-00-223584-6

I. Title.

PS8503.U36P98 1991   C813'.54   C90-093795-5
PR9199.3.B84P98 1991

91 92 93 94 95 OFF 5 4 3 2 1

PYX (pĭks), *noun*. **1.** the vessel, case or tabernacle in which the Host is reserved. **2.** The little vessel, usually watch-shaped, in which the Eucharist is carried to the sick.

— *Webster's New International*

1
THE PRESENT

A little after one, Jack Trudel turned his cab into Hillton Road and began to drive slowly down its slope. The residential apartments always impressed him, they seemed unbelievably big, full of massive pleasures. They made permanent what Trudel thought was happiness. He didn't know anything about it; he had read the cheap novels, the scandal sheets, and dreamed of money. The mild bitterness he felt was enjoyable, and the sight of the stolid apartments, dimly seen in the street light and the spill of his headlights, gave him something real about which to dream.

It was hot. And the rain hadn't changed the temperature, it had only added the dampness. The streets still glistened in spots. Trudel's radio sputtered with calls for someone else. He didn't want a call just then, he was imagining himself in an air-conditioned apartment on Hillton Road; and his intention was to pull up and think about it a little.

It was then that he saw it, just past the glaring glass entrance to the biggest apartment on the street. Something that looked mainly white fell fast to the sidewalk and was still. The noise it made was sharp but not clangy, like a block of wood hitting the cement. His foot was on the brake before his reverie was broken. Realization didn't set in until he began edging the car forward, riding the clutch, sitting upright, sweating unaware of the heat. He saw shoes, a woman's shoes, what looked like an evening dress, legs twisted, a white face....He stopped the car.

He sank back in the seat. He felt chilly. He opened the door of the car and vomited on the street. When he straightened and saw that his hands were shaking, he held on to the steering wheel. After a while he reached for the microphone on the dash.

"Mike," he said weakly to the dispatcher.

"Who's calling?" demanded the metallic voice.

"Mike, it's Trudel...."

"Yeah."

"...I'm on Hillton Road, down from Ellesbry..."

"OK, I'll contact you if I get a call."

"Mike, get the cops."

"You in trouble?"

"Yeah, somebody jumped off a building."

He put back the microphone, careful not to look at the person on the sidewalk. He lit a cigarette after two attempts, and smoked trying to get warm again. A dream had vanished forever.

He didn't remember if his brakes had screeched, or if he had accidentally pressed his horn, but almost immediately people appeared to see what had happened. A car unloaded a group of good-timers: three men and three

3

women, all young. Another cab stopped, the driver was paid and the customer got out to see; the driver stayed. Windows opened. Lights came on in houses along the street.

"You hit her?" said one good-timer, a fleshy handsome type with wet eyes. His companion looked at Trudel's headlights. Trudel didn't answer. He blew smoke at the windshield.

"Don't touch anything," a voice said. A few giggles arose from the girls. Someone was sick, more people arrived, the muttering rose into confused questioning and debate, and Trudel sighed as a siren jelled the tragedy into manageable proportions. He turned off his headlights and silence fell on the growing crowd for a moment.

Henderson lifted a corner of the red blanket and looked at the dead woman. A few people edged in closer.

"Young," he murmured to the man with him. He himself was in his fifties, balding and greying, with a tall, heavy, now paunchy body. He looked up at the uniformed policeman and said, "She's wearing an evening dress. Any signs of a party?"

"No sir," said the policeman, "nobody around but the taxi driver when it happened."

The street was blocked with cars and people; the activity had attracted the night life. The cars, unable to pass easily, accumulated from two directions and added to the congestion as their occupants got out to see. An ambulance had forced its way through, but it returned immediately. The police were clearing the far side of the street by having a squad car drive through hinting with its siren. People moved slowly in the heat; the still curious crowded the sidewalk where she lay, others stood across the street, vaguely incredulous: they would believe their senses when they read about it in the papers. A few were angry at the disturbance. A reporter sat in his car looking ready to leave: it was a small item, just another suicide: but she may have come from an important family, the family might make a story.

Henderson pointed to the large leather handbag at her side.

"Was that like that when you got here?"

"No sir, it was about twenty feet from the body. I moved it and covered it."

"You the only one who touched it?"

"As far as I know, yes. When I asked they said they were too scared to touch it. One man said he nudged it with his foot."

Henderson opened the handbag and removed a wallet. He shook powder from it—a compact had burst open—and found a driver's licence and a car registration for a Lincoln made out to Elizabeth Lucy of 88 Rotsley Avenue. He looked for car keys in the purse and found none. The other detective, a thin young dark-haired man named Cerini, looked at the registration and went to find the apartment garage. Henderson continued looking through her things, but saw only the usual personal equipment, no letters, no note, no address book; he took out a ring holding four house keys, put the bag down and sought out the cab driver.

As he was listening to Trudel's account, people gathered round him. "Did he do it?" a voice said; they expected to see an arrest. Henderson moved into the cab and closed the door.

"You didn't see the actual fall?"

"No, just when she hit."

"How much of the building could you see?"

"Well, I wasn't looking there till I noticed something. I was a few feet back of here."

"Move the car back to where you were."

Eventually—the surrounding group thought he wanted to move ahead—Trudel edged the car back. By straining forward and turning his head up, Henderson could make out the top of the building. He counted over ten stories but the light was poor.

"After it happened, did you see anyone leave the building?"

"No, I didn't. But I don't think I would have noticed anyway. It shook me up a bit. You know, I never seen anyone...." He had no more to say.

The morgue truck was arriving, and Henderson went to meet it. The crowd tightened around it with renewed interest, but the driver and the attendant worked swiftly, and without removing the blanket they strapped the body to a metal stretcher and placed it in the panel truck. It belonged to the coroner now, the crowd had nothing but the traces on the sidewalk. Henderson spoke to the attendant who wrote down what concerned him, and finally the black truck pulled away and ended the spectacle.

Slowly the crowd and the cars thinned out. Henderson dismissed the second police car, the cab driver was allowed to go; the street returned to its residential quiet, and the hot night air grew noticeable once more.

"No Lincoln with that number in the garage," said Cerini. He indicated the man who was with him. "This is the manager. Edgar Poulin." Poulin was a short, smooth man; he had dressed fully to come out, white shirt, tie, jacket, and his hair combed.

Henderson nodded, "You were up when this happened?"

"Oh, no," said Poulin, "I was asleep. The noise of the cars woke me up. I got dressed and came out. It's an awful thing."

"Did you recognize the girl?"

"No, never saw her before. She wasn't a tenant here."

"You're sure of that?"

"Why yes."

"She could have been living here," said Henderson.

"Not without my knowing it."

"Do you check on your tenants' girl friends?"

Poulin didn't answer. Henderson had the policeman shine a light on the building.

"How many stories there, Mr. Poulin?"

"Eleven, and a penthouse."

"Metal windows," said Cerini, "all screened and closed."

Henderson noticed that the line of descent did not coincide with the windows.

"Who lives in the penthouse?" he asked.

"A Mr. Keerson."

"Has he been in tonight?"

"I wouldn't know. I've never seen him. I never go up there."

"Isn't that a little unusual?"

"No. Around here people buy privacy."

"We'll have to have a look in there anyway."

"Look," said Poulin, "I'm not supposed to go up there. I wouldn't have a key except for fire regulations. It'd cost me my job to use it, it's strictly for emergencies."

"That's what this is," said Cerini, and he walked into the main entrance.

After Henderson rang and tried the four keys he had taken from her purse, Poulin let them in and waited outside. They were in a long wide hall, heavily carpeted, that ran the length of the penthouse. There were doors on either side, and on the right another hall.

9

Cerini turned into it and said, "The front's this way."

They passed through high glass doors and on to the terrace. Henderson looked at the edge of the building, the terrace floor, the area in line with the doors; there was nothing to be seen.

The city glowed from below and in the distance. The night lights made the sky red, and the dust made it look opaque. Clouds still hovered in the damp heat. Henderson watched Hillton Road turn gently through its residential area and disappear downtown where the light was stronger. Faint traffic sounds drifted to the height; the two cars below looked inoffensive in the empty street; what had happened was now memory, straining to be forgotten altogether.

"It must've been from here," said Henderson. "There's no other place to drop from."

"Nice high spot," said Cerini. "When she's had enough of living, she gets all dressed up, comes up here, and jumps. At least she didn't do it downtown at five o'clock."

Henderson looked at the city.

"Somebody must've let her in," he said. "We didn't find a key."

"Maybe she threw it away."

"Why bother with that? She didn't bother with anything else. She even took her purse along."

They examined the terrace again but found nothing.

"Good place for a party," said Cerini.

"No signs of it."

"There must be some connection between her and the guy that lives here."

"There doesn't have to be. Maybe he's in a heart-breaking business. Let's try inside."

The living room was on the side of the penthouse away from the terrace. It was large, taking in what looked like the whole side wall; it contained several sofas, a number of odd-shaped chairs, islands of coffee tables, and a floor that was all rug. Three walls held paintings meaningless to Henderson, and scattered around the room on tables and ornate little shelves were statuettes that years ago would have made him blush, bits of abstract sculpturing, misshapen candle holders, and a variety of vases. The fourth wall was covered by drapes which Cerini drew open to reveal more glass doors, full-length windows, and another terrace. At one end of the room on a low dais was

11

a long carved table of dark wood with a canopy over it and fixed drapes behind it. On the side of the table, Henderson found a small plaque that read "Eugenio di Callitiere, 1852."

"Do you suppose he eats off this?" said Cerini.

"Maybe it's a sales gimmick."

They looked through the rest of the rooms, but found no signs of recent living. In the kitchen, the refrigerator was running; it contained food that could have been there for a week. They returned to the living room and stood there looking.

"There's no dust on anything," said Henderson, "the ash trays are clean."

"And it's nice and cool," said Cerini, flatly, "the air-conditioning is on."

They found vents over the long windows and the control mechanism on the wall behind the fixed drapes. Henderson looked at it and pressed a switch. A vague whirring indicated that he had turned it on. He stopped it and said, "Somebody turned this off not so long ago."

They both knew it proved nothing.

"Maybe Keerson can tell us something when we see him," said Cerini.

"He doesn't have to. All she did was use his penthouse. Maybe her folks can tell us more."

As they were leaving, Henderson noticed that the phone had no number in the center of its dial.

A few minutes after they had gone, a cab stopped down the street; Jack Trudel got out and walked until from across the street he could see the spot where the woman had died. The tall apartments impressed him more than before; the image he had of ease and pleasant power had now acquired a background of horror. He stood there smoking, a puzzled frown on his face. Guys get beat up in back lanes, and thrown in the river, people run under trains, and drunks smash up cars full of people, but women in evening dresses who live around here don't...but she did. Maybe she doesn't live around here. She doesn't live anywhere now, she doesn't even live. Real violence was too much for him; in the cheap stories, he could always dream of sex; but the actual thing....Already he was beginning to dismiss it as outside the real course of life.

As he threw his butt into the street, something like a coin caught his eye, and drew him like a ringing phone. He picked up what looked like a gold locket with a broken chain. He snapped it open expecting a picture of someone, maybe of...But there was no picture, just a place for one, a circular depression about an inch in diameter. He thought it probably belonged to one of the girls who gaped at him before the police arrived. His mind now totally absorbed in how much he could get for it, he went back to his car and drove off.

Rotsley Avenue was a downtown street that began with the side of a department store and continued with former three-story homes converted into commercial buildings and boarding houses. One of these had been turned into a club called the Evening Star. At the end of the street was number 88, an apartment building. It still bore a real estate sign announcing its high-priced suites. A few lights were on. Henderson looked at the parked cars, but none was a Lincoln. After trying the garage, which was locked, he and Cerini went into the main entrance.

The row of names on the wall didn't have an Elizabeth Lucy. Henderson rang at "H. Worther, Supt. 1A," and they went downstairs to the apartment. No one answered. Henderson knocked loudly. Finally a man opened the door.

"What is it?" he asked angrily. He was big and too heavy, his weight strained his yellow and mauve T-shirt. A radio was on. He had been drinking.

"Police," said Henderson, and the man's eyes became alert.

"What's the trouble?"

"Nothing. We want to locate somebody."

"Not here, this is a high-class place."

"So is the person we want to locate."

"Well, if that's the..." His voice dwindled as he caught the irony. "Who?" he snapped.

"Is there an Elizabeth Lucy living here?"

The man didn't answer. He looked wearily from Henderson to Cerini, trying to adjust his thoughts.

Then he said, "I wouldn't know. The list of names is out front."

"We know," said Henderson. "Does she live here?"

"Like I said, this is a high-class place. I don't want cops all over the building. It's bad for the reputation."

Henderson said, "Keep him here," and walked down the hall and through a large door which led him to the garage. After a brief search, he found a blue Lincoln with the right licence plates; there were a few rain spots on it. The keys were in the ignition. He turned it on and looked at the temperature gauge; it was cold. He looked in the trunk and found nothing. He took the keys and went back to 1A.

"The car's there," he said to Cerini. "Look, Worther, we're going to start ringing doorbells."

"Alright, alright," Worther barked, and added in a lower tone, "number 10, Mrs. Latimer's apartment. But she's not there now, so you don't have to go up."

"Who's not there?"

"Miss Lucy."

"How do you know she's not there?"

Worther hesitated. "I didn't see her come back."

"Do you watch for her?"

The man was visibly uncomfortable.

"We're...friends," he muttered. "We talk every now and then."

"Was that car out tonight?"

"Dunno."

"You see her leave?"

"No."

"How do you know she's out?"

"She's always out. She's always back late. Hell, you get to know your tenants."

"Yeah, if you wait up late enough."

They left him.

They rang at apartment number 10 and waited. It was 2:30 in the morning, they expected to wait. Vague sounds came through the door, too vague to identify as grunts or movements. Henderson rang again. A muffled but excited voice sounded inside, and then a slight tinkle, the sound a phone sometimes makes when the receiver is replaced. Henderson knocked on the door this time.

"Who is it?" a woman's voice asked.

Henderson didn't answer.

"Our boy downstairs calling," Cerini whispered, "just a loyal friend."

The door opened as far as the chain would let it. What was visible of the face that looked out of the opening was carefully made up and stiffened in an age that could have been anywhere from forty to sixty. The brown hair was well done in a sort of formal youthfulness that didn't match the eyes that looked at them, eyes that knew they were looking at detectives.

"Yes?" she said.

"Mrs. Latimer?" said Henderson.

She nodded slowly.

"We're police, we'd like to talk to you."

"What about?" She didn't move.

"We could talk better inside," said Henderson pleasantly.

"Let's hear it outside first."

"One of the girls living here, Elizabeth Lucy, she died tonight. Get that chain off the door." He was still speaking pleasantly, but his lips hardly moved, and his eyes insisted where his voice hadn't.

She closed the door, slipped off the chain and opened it wide. They followed her through a small hall into the living room. It was well furnished but cluttered: knick-knacks and frills, vases, fancy cups on delicate little shelves, figurines, four abstract paintings, gags in picture frames, an apartment piano, a hi-fi set, tables, cigarette humidors, ashtrays of all shapes, lighters, anything that could be there normally, anything advertised as expensive or exclusive, anything buyable, anything, it struck Henderson, that could make a search of the place about as easy as finding the molecule that set off an explosion.

She sat down on a couch that looked square, reached for a cigarette, and sat back, silent.

"How well did you know this Lucy girl?" Henderson asked.

"Not very well, she just lived here."

"Can you tell us who her folks are?"

"No."

"What other people live here?"

"Two other girls."

"Working girls?"

"Yes."

"What kind of work?"

"They're entertainers."

"This Elizabeth Lucy was an entertainer too?"

"Yes."

"And what do you do, Mrs. Latimer?"

"I keep house for them."

Henderson looked at the expensively kept hair, the expert make-up, the manicured hands, the clothes that weren't house clothes.

"What club did she work at?"

"They...she hasn't been doing clubs lately, private parties mainly."

"Is that where she went tonight?"

"I don't know."

"Did she leave from here?"

She waited awhile and smoked. Then she nodded yes.

"What time did she leave?"

"About 10 or 11, I'm not sure."

"How was she dressed?"

"She had on a pale green dress, close-fitting."

"Handbag?"

"Yes."

"Go on," said Henderson.

"Go on with what?"

"What kind of handbag?"

"Large, brown leather."

"Did she take her car?"

"I don't know."

"Nobody called for her?"

"No."

Henderson didn't say anything for a while. He was used to lies, used to sifting through them, not for truth, but for stray information. Cerini was getting impatient.

Henderson said, "Was she carrying anything else, something that could have held an evening dress?"

"Evening dress. Why an evening dress?"

"She died in one."

She put out her cigarette and lit another. She smoked it sitting forward on the couch.

"How...how did she die?" She didn't look at Henderson when she spoke.

"On Hillton Road, there's an eleven-story apartment with a penthouse. She came down from there." Henderson saw that she was keeping herself under control; he kept talking. "She was young, beautiful I suppose, and she was making lots of money, at least it looks that way. She was going to a party, a private party, and she ends up dead. She may have killed herself. What do you think, Mrs. Latimer?"

"I haven't a thing to tell you." Her voice was strained and her eyes glistened and the way she spoke was full of fear. "Just go away, she's dead."

Henderson stood up. "I'd like to see her room," he said. Cerini left immediately to look around. "She may have left a note. Maybe some letters that'll tell us who her family is."

"She didn't get any mail. And she didn't write any letters."

"She must have been a lonely girl."

"Yes, I suppose she was."

"Where's her room?"

She led the way. Henderson's first impression was that it looked like a hotel room. It was orderly, the bed was made and covered, the dresser wasn't cluttered. The clothes closet contained about a dozen dresses—none of them pale green—night clothes, shoes, hats, a few boxes. He opened the dresser drawers and found nothing unusual, except that there wasn't much of anything. From a drawer he removed a picture of the girl; it was a head-and-shoulders shot, taken outdoors. He indicated to Mrs. Latimer that he was keeping it.

"An entertainer would have large glossy prints. Any of those around?"

"No."

Henderson thought the room was too neat, but he didn't say anything. If she had been getting ready to commit suicide, she could have performed any number of meaningless rituals. If not....They went back to the living room.

Henderson played with the photograph and said, "I suppose you'll be down to claim the body."

Mrs. Latimer looked at him, her eyes were disturbed this time.

"No," she said, "the girls can identify her."

Henderson turned the picture over, there was nothing on the back. If she hadn't been in touch with anybody, it would be a long time before anyone missed her and started asking about her: she was not only dead, it was as if she had never existed. He decided to probe a little deeper.

"She worked for you," he said, "you probably owe her a lot."

"Nothing was said about her working for me."

"I know. But I can add. Who are the other two girls that live here?"

"What do you want with them?"

"They may know something about her."

"One's Marie, the other's Sue. They wouldn't know anything about her."

"No, but they might know something about you."

"She lived here. That's all I know. That's all they know."

They looked at her, not saying anything. She was very nervous now. She went to the door and opened it.

"You can't touch me," she said, almost in a whisper. "She killed herself, it's all over. There's nothing here for you."

They walked out, and the door was locked after them. Henderson thought he heard her crying behind it, but he couldn't be sure if he had only wished it.

They got into the car, Cerini drove. The streets were empty of normal activity; only the late celebrants made noises; the cars they rode in seemed driverless. The lights still proclaimed an accessible paradise, they preened themselves in gay patterns, they blinked on and off, they blared, they flared in bright obvious colors announcing either business or pleasure. They had more energy than people, but there were lots of people in a big city. Now, the lights were just lights, a little out of place, like a lonely waiter announcing a last call for dinner on an empty moving train.

Cerini didn't say anything, they both knew the meaning of the night's events. They were used to the swirl of the city in a way, a desperate way, like a man would get used to drowning if he could repeat the process. They knew the pattern; they had only to wait to see it emerge, to watch for the rarely original features of evil.

It didn't concern Henderson personally, he was only a detective. Someone had to ascertain the manner of her dying. She wasn't a relative, a friend, an acquaintance, she probably wasn't even a name in the police file. He knew nothing

THE PYX

about her, and she was nothing to him save a dead human being. Yet the violence of her dying, the place, and the silence and the evasion following it, all this was now his knowledge. He felt, because he was, a stranger hired to be human enough to feel the tragedy of her ending.

Henderson's face glistened in the warm office. He sat leaning forward in a wooden armchair and looked at the things on the table in front of him. A noisy fan moved the air around and pushed the smoke out the window. It had become cooler as the night grew older, but not cool enough. He wiped his face slowly, his mind on the things before him.

The handbag was open and had been emptied. Next to it was a wallet, also empty, forty-two dollars and eighty-three cents in a neat pile, a driver's licence, a registration, the car keys he had taken from the car, a ring of four house keys to which he had fastened a tag, make-up, a small pack of tissues, two theatre tickets, three photographs, a swizzle-stick from a club called the Evening Star, a sheer hanky, sun-glasses, a long thin lighter defined for ladies in the advertisements.

One of the photographs was of a group of four women at the beach, none of them Mrs. Latimer. Another was of a group at a table, the girl was in it with an older man at her side, his arm paternally around her shoulders. Two other couples rounded off the party: the old boys laughed leeringly and the women mechanically. The third picture, which had been in a different section of the wallet, was of a man about fifty or sixty, tired-looking in a strong man's way, of good posture, standing on house steps to a gallery and waving good-bye at the camera. He wasn't smiling. On the back was the rubber-stamp name "Marc Lapier, photos."

Henderson fingered the licence. The name "Lucy" was phoney, of course, a trade name. Still, you never know. He sat back and lit a cigarette. He stared at the fan and blew smoke at it and watched the swirls. People who are going to commit suicide don't plan on going to the theatre. Who said she was planning to go to the theatre? Maybe somebody dumped them on her, maybe some flush lad who owned a piece of everything. Say she was planning on going to the theatre, it doesn't mean a thing. A man could plan an elaborate trip, make all the reservations, say all the good-byes, and then, feeling that that won't get him away from it all, could cut his throat in the airport toilet. The tickets prove nothing. Nothing proves nothing. She jumped and that's all there is to it. The man in the penthouse probably just likes to make mysteries, or is shy with policemen, or had to run off and hit the bottle. Maybe he'll call up and apologize. Most likely he doesn't even know it happened.

He broke his train of thought and stood up in the stream of the fan.

Cerini came in and sat down opposite Henderson's vacated chair.

"Did you see this?" he said.

Henderson went to the desk. Cerini picked up the handbag. It was of heavily embossed leather. He pushed the flap all the way over and showed that the embossing covered up a small pocket lined with felt.

"They found a small hypo in here. All ready to go. Heroin."

Henderson examined the handbag. It was just a gesture.

"Anything on her in the file?" he asked.

"Nothing," said Cerini, "nice, smart, clean-living hustler."

27

"No jokes, it's too hot."

"Leroux says the fall caused the death. She was an addict and probably loaded. And that's all there is to it. He'll confirm it all tomorrow."

"Gets all dressed up for private kicks," said Henderson, "and then jumps. Could be. But we need keys to the Hillton Road place, and the clothes she was wearing before she changed to the evening dress."

"Funny thing about that evening dress. It wasn't an ordinary dress like you'd see at a ball. Leroux says it's more like you'd see at a ballet or in the movies."

"So it's a style to liven up a party."

"Might be, because she had nothing else on."

"I'm shocked," said Henderson.

Cerini laughed. "Something else," he said. "You never can tell about these things. She falls twelve stories and bangs the sidewalk and keeps a rose in her hair."

"Yeah," said Henderson. "It happens all the time."

Henderson went to the morgue alone. Leroux, the assistant coroner, had gone home, and the attendant, who was getting ready to put the body away, left it for Henderson. An overhead light shone clearly on him and on the draped body of the girl on the long table. He was vaguely aware of the other tables and the barely lit rows of large drawers in the wall opposite him. It was cool, and silent. He didn't feel his tiredness, but his mind was overworking, running on with the events, waiting for the right fact to settle on. But no right fact appeared. Here she was. That seemed to be fact enough.

She was a beautiful girl, looking younger now than she probably was. Her face was intact. They had removed the make-up, and death had taken away whatever else was there, pain perhaps, and certainly the personality that once animated it. Her hair was a blend of blond and auburn resting on the part of the sheet that had been pulled around to hide the base of her head. Her eyes were closed, and Henderson thought of the clichés about sleep and calmness; he grunted as he pictured the real violence behind it all. Nobody will claim this body, he thought. At least not now, not until he or some other detective found the friend or the relative who would care enough to bury it. Worther or Mrs. Latimer would want the body, but alive,

alive to peddle it, to feed it heroin, to dress it up, to make it entertain lechers who had nothing but money and erotic energy, to make it stop belonging to a human being, to make it wind up here with a long jump, or a long push.

He rubbed the back of his neck. Soft, he said without a sound. Then he answered himself, no, you're not getting soft, you were never hard. It wasn't that death upset him. He had seen it undressed and violent, he had delivered it a few times, he had watched it officially, but always with a sense of its immensity, its impressive finality.

Another hustler dies, a hustler on the needle. The city's full of it, any city. The morgue boys pick them up and throw them in a common grave. And that's life. Leave the humanity out of it, it got itself left out a long time ago. Forget it. Stick to the facts. Leroux'll tell you tomorrow if she was too drugged to stand; if so, she fell; if not, she jumped. Make the report, there's no humanity in a report.

And under the ceiling light, he looked at her face again. Leave it out, he thought; there's nothing else but humanity, the whole mess is human.

He crossed the room to another smaller table.

He clicked on the lamp that was on it. A rose and a crumpled and stained evening dress were there. He sat down, lit a cigarette, and leaned back in the chair letting his ideas drift with the smoke. He became aware of the silence and the one ceiling light. He reached over and fingered the so-called evening dress. It was made of sheer material but lots of it, so that it could be draped in many folds. It was no peepshow nightgown. Somebody went in for the erotic in a big way. The finale must have been something to see. The dress, the handbag, the rose, that was all. In a dress like that, you wouldn't go on the street; if you did, you'd be wearing something over it. But even if you were wearing something over it, why bring a large handbag? The needle could be carried in a smaller purse. And if you had the handbag, that means that when you left home you weren't in the sheer get-up. Mrs. Latimer was careful about that one; a green dress she said, she was right about the dress. He smoked and stared at the things. If she took her own car and her street clothes and went someplace to commit suicide, the car and the clothes would still be there. Unless someone would be very embarrassed by the suicide, someone who didn't want dead hustlers on his hands even if they were unmurdered, someone with a fussy taste in sex, someone with power who could get cars back and clothes removed, someone nice and gentle who liked roses.

He got up and put the desk light off. He went back to the long table taking the rose with him. He held it as a focal point for his thoughts and let smoke exhale with his breathing. Then he laughed once, curtly. "Fine thing," he said aloud, "keeping vigil with a dead girl and a flower." He walked away, called the attendant, and left with the flower in his shirt pocket.

2
THE PAST

They had gone at 6 A.M. in a yellow Cadillac, promising she'd hear from them; three of them, well-fed, loud-mouthed, hard with power and the delusion of it, and sentimental, at least about women like her: You're a real sport, kitten, they sure know how to grow them in this town. The sentimentality, she knew, was confined to hotel rooms and quick-rent apartments; three blocks away and ten minutes later they wouldn't recognize her. The other girls had gone before her, they never left in a group; and so she had remained for the good-byes, the raucous cheerfulness from the front seat of the yellow car. They had gone; they always go, back to their businesses, their paper empires, their wives, back to themselves. One could always count on that: it always ended, the time arrived, they left.

Elizabeth Lucy felt free for the moment; their leaving early gave her a little time, and just being rid of them was good. But a sense of unreality soured whatever joy she could have felt. She decided to walk a few blocks; and as soon as she started, she realized she was very tired. The morning air was cool, and the sun had risen just enough to light up things in a grey rain-like color. That early in the morning, the derelicts look for things in the streets, walking, to avoid the active attention of the police; a few cabs ride about; workmen sit on buses with lunch pails, even on that morning which was Sunday. The men she passed looked at her; it was always more than a passing glance. She hardly noticed them, nothing seemed worth noticing. She felt, not cut off, but far away from what was around her; the street was just a street, the sun was just happening, the people existed like a radio you've forgotten was on, and her walking was motion that she wanted to stop soon.

She went two blocks to one of the city's main intersections. The restaurant on the corner looked open; she decided on a cup of coffee before getting her car. She had parked it at an all-night garage. A smile almost reached her face as she thought of Meg Latimer insisting that they not take their cars where they went: the men feel you're competing with them, and the cheap ones take advantage.

At the far end of the restaurant, an old man was carefully mopping the floor, somewhere in the back someone typed erratically, and in front a man about thirty-five was stacking dishes on the glass shelves. As she walked to the counter, he saw her through the mirror behind the shelves, a quick glance at first that turned him around to tell her the place was still closed. But then he saw the warm gold-rust hair, and the eyes that looked perhaps green, and what showed of her tall body in the expensive summer dress. He nodded.

She said very quietly, "Coffee, please," and sat down at a table. A while ago, perhaps years, she would have noticed his action and smiled, enjoying the effect she had. She might even have helped it a little. But now, she couldn't be pleased or flattered by her beauty; it wasn't part of her consciousness; it was just a fact, a thing that was part of her life, something others thought she was lucky enough to have, something others wanted. She had no mental picture of herself as an outwardly visible person; she had only an inner vision of...

"Here's your coffee, Miss."

He put it down gently, and took the money, trying to look as if he hadn't. He hesitated just long enough to suppress a "you feeling alright, lady?" and went back to his work; he was old enough not to get involved.

She drank some of the coffee; he had done his best with it, but it wasn't very good; it wasn't coffee she needed. The light outside was becoming sunlight: another inverted day; she would go home eventually, and sleep, or try to; then a day, perhaps a few days, of idleness that should be rest. Formerly she could get some enjoyment out of buying things, wearing good clothes, driving her car, going places, sharing the assumed happiness of the others; but all these were meaningless gestures now. For her, reality was otherwise; it was the work, the habit, the growing depression—none of them alterable.

More people were beginning to appear outside, traffic was a little busier. Her watch said quarter to seven. She finished the coffee, put on some sunglasses, and went outside. She walked two blocks to a large entrance under a still lit neon sign that said "Kentshire Parking" and went in to get her car. She had a little time: Meg Latimer would know when the other girls had gone, but she wouldn't know how long it took the party to break up fully. Even at that, you didn't lie to Meg.

The place she drove to was a four-story building with about twenty windows showing to a floor. It had a wide lawn, the length of several city blocks, and part of a playground showed from the side of the building. It was all enclosed by a low retaining wall that held a seven-foot iron fence with pickets like dull spears, but it looked small compared to the big maples that grew out of the well-kept lawn and flanked the driveway. The metal gates were closed, but she knew they didn't lock them. She left the car idling and swung them open. She drove along

the circular driveway, parked on one side of the
stone steps, and went up to the polished doors.
She pressed a buzzer and tried to see through
the frosted glass design. By the time she had her
sunglasses off, a stout, businesslike woman in a
pale blue uniform opened the door.

"I would like to see Dr. Hildebrand."

The stout woman looked at her with a knowing eye that softened into envy and hardened
into disapproval. The eye went to the torso of the
summer dress, to the car in the driveway, all very
fast, curious, full of something that wasn't strong
enough to be hate; it was disappointed; it had
guessed the obvious perhaps, but hadn't seen
anything God could punish. She led the way into
a waiting room and left without saying a word.

Alone, she didn't sit down. She had a
cigarette going before she looked for an ashtray,
but she found one, and smiled at the idea of Dr.
Hildebrand getting the stout woman or someone like her to put an ashtray in the waiting
room. The room was large, with a high ceiling
and windows taller than a door. Around the
wall was an assortment of chairs, some padded
and stiff like an old-time minuet. The windows
had white, clean, billowy curtains; the rug was

old but confirmed in its neatness; a big plant
rested on a three-legged stand built decoratively
to accommodate it. The wall opposite the windows bore a large colored picture of the bishop,
and further, on each side, two prints of obvious
masterpieces looking lonely in this century.

She heard someone coming and turned to see
a nun enter the room. She was short and wiry
and walked quickly. That air of energy and her
pink unpainted face made her look young; the
smile made her look even younger; but about an
inch of grey hair showed where her headgear
began. Her eyes were clear, as though she slept
well, and the lines around them gave her an
atmosphere of amused candor.

"Hello, Miss Lucy," she said, "won't you sit
down?"

The nun brought a chair to the table, but
Elizabeth kept standing.

"Doctor," she said, "I want to see Sandra. Do
you think I could?"

Dr. Hildebrand sat down slowly.

"Miss Lucy," she said, "I know what this means
to you and I'm willing to let you see her. But she
couldn't speak to you in a normal manner."

"It's that hard."

"It *is* very difficult. There's no doubt about that. For three weeks, or three months, sometimes even longer, she'll suffer a great deal. We can't give her much relief because we prefer not to use drugs. We can only give her a little comfort. She knows we're helping her. She's very brave. She's young and there are no psychiatric complications."

"She's eighteen. I suppose an older addict, I mean someone who had been addicted longer, a person like that would have more trouble."

Dr. Hildebrand appeared to take the question academically. She thought it over and replied: "That's usually true. Time makes a difference. But then so does the degree of dosage."

"Being young helps."

"You're not so old," said Dr. Hildebrand and her eyes looked as if she had said it was a fine day. All she was supposed to know was that Elizabeth had brought a young girl called Sandra to her hospital. The world outside didn't know there was a Sandra or a Dr. Hildebrand.

"No," said Elizabeth, "but there are other things."

"I'll take you to her," said the doctor, standing, "but you mustn't try to talk to her."

They left the waiting room and made their way to the back of the building and up to the second floor. They stopped at a white door marked "29" and Dr. Hildebrand motioned Elizabeth to stay at the door. Then she went through it and left it open.

A blonde girl sat Indian fashion on the bed, shivering, her head drooping forward and her hands stroking the back of her neck and hair. Books were strewn on the floor and a chair was upset in one corner and the wall above it was marked and dented. The shade was drawn most of the way. There were sunglasses on her night table next to a vase of roses.

"Sandra."

Dr. Hildebrand spoke quietly. The girl stopped moving her hands but didn't look up.

"The sun came up hours ago," she said in a high, weak voice, "and it still isn't day. Why, why does it take so long, Sister?"

"That's the way it feels, Sandra," the nun answered, "as if you're functioning faster than time. It'll go the right way again. You might even want to slow it up when you're happy."

The girl cried, and the sobs threatened to rise.

"Do you like your flowers?"

A memory stirred, an important memory.

"They smell funny," the girl said.

"Yes, they usually do for a while."

"What was that animal doing in the field out there? It was like a horse. But it wasn't a horse. It was...It had..."

"That must have been a cow, Sandra."

"How did it get there?"

"Well, our order has an orphanage on this land. They farm a little. A resident farmer does the heavy work. But they're thinking of getting rid of the cows."

The girl laughed, again with the threat of lost control.

"What would they want," the laughter got higher, "with the silly things anyway?"

The candor in Dr. Hildebrand made her say, "They give milk."

Arid the girl stopped laughing. She looked up, frightened.

"They don't really, do they, do they? You're just fooling, aren't you? You're just making a joke; that can't be, about the cow, you're just fooling, I mean...."

Again the candor said, "No, Sandra, cows give milk, people pasteurize it, put it up in bottles and sell it to those who want it."

The girl sobbed so badly that Dr. Hildebrand sat on the bed and held her in her arms. After a while, between diminishing sobs, the girl said, "I never knew that, Sister, I never really knew where milk came from. You'll show me, eh, how it's done. There must be a hundred million things I thought people made that aren't made at all. That is, aren't made by people at least. I mean...."

"I know what you mean."

Reassured, the girl cried into the whiteness of Dr. Hildebrand's habit. When she stopped, she said, "I love you, Sister."

"I love you too, Sandra."

She kissed the girl's hair and left the room.

She and Elizabeth didn't talk till they were at the front door. Then Elizabeth said, "For certain things, I have courage, Doctor, but this is not one of them."

"Right now, as we stand here, there's no need for courage. It only comes when it's needed."

"I suppose she's still crying," said Elizabeth, "she started again as we walked down the hall, you know."

"I know."

"I have to go. I can't be seen here. Good-bye, Doctor. And thanks."

She drove hurriedly away in the deserted
street and got to a busier section. She looked
anxiously at her watch: 7:25. She parked the car
and sat there. She tried hard to adopt an artifi-
cial calmness, but the tension and the panic
made her burst into tears. There was no turning
back for her, no Dr. Hildebrand to take her
through the agony, no someone to take her to
the right hospital, no hopeful circumstances.
She already knew that milk wasn't brewed like
paint; she couldn't hope for such a primal innocence; she couldn't hope for anything. Meg
Latimer was her Dr. Hildebrand.

A car pulled up alongside hers and all but
stopped. When she saw color she knew it
wasn't the police. Without turning her head,
she started the engine and made it roar. As she
was peering along the hood as though looking
for clearance, the other car drove off. She could
see two brightly colored summer caps and
thick necks in the convertible ahead, golf clubs
looking out of the back seat, two thick necks
red with the sun and high blood pressure,
made all the more apparent by the close-
cropped white hair. She turned off the ignition.
Sorry boys, it'll have to be golf, it's a good

game, gives you lots of time to look at the girls.
Again, she hadn't realized the effect of her
appearance: hair the color of candle-light filter-
ing a sunset, a profile that was all female, the
touch of sexiness added by the sunglasses and
the make-up, the car. In other circumstances,
entering a nightclub with an obvious escort,
going with another girl to an address Meg gave
them, seen in what was referred to as a party of
four or six or whatever number even or odd
that happened, seen that way, she made men
stop and wonder if there was a mistake, and
impressed them with delight when it became
clear that there was no mistake. Beauty under
those circumstances was merely an additive.
But away from that, in the street, the theatre, a
restaurant, the beach, everywhere else, people
looked at her and thought better of humanity.

The car didn't offer much privacy; it made
her public, and made her tears public for anyone who got close enough to see. She didn't
trust herself to drive at that moment, but she
wanted to go somewhere, not Meg's, where she
could regain a measure of control. She got out,
and locked the car. She thought confusedly
about a place to go to; a bar at this hour would

bring knowing looks, a hotel lobby too, the theatres weren't open. She walked. It was an effort to walk well, not to hurry nervously, not to make things worse in the heat of the growing day. She crossed a street against the traffic light.

On her right, she became aware of a large lawn with a cement walk that led to huge doors. She took it, went up the stone steps, and through a large wooden door into the dark and intermittently lit cathedral.

It was cool inside, and private, as anonymous as a railroad station. She sat down in a pew near the back beside a pillar the size of a small room. At the front, what looked like a dozen people in that immense building, and was probably fifty, attended a silent mass; she couldn't have been more alone in an empty theatre. No curious cars here, no anticipating looks, no hungry eyes: the external pressure was gone; but she still had herself and what the self knew. She closed her eyes, waiting for some hint of repose, the shadow of approaching peace: would peace be a shadow, a part of the darkness?...Closing her eyes didn't bring peace, that was hoping for too much, what came instead was the picture of Sandra, the shock of it dulled by her half-dozing state, but the horror clear and unblurred; it took on an energy of its own and oppressed her with fear. Fear created images, not like pictures, but like knowledges. She put her hand to her head and rubbed her brow which was wet. Then as her tiredness overran her consciousness, the image of Meg Latimer arose, a smile, fixed at first then growing, the false teeth grew grey like steel but alive like tired reptiles, and became a wriggling trap like rich, damp, sickly swamp vegetation, in the center of which was whiteness, a whiteness that shattered into fine powder, dissolved in the dampness and was about to give her peace but a monstrous needle replaced it all and changed into a black icicle held in a frozen hand that rested on the entire length of a hospital bed once occupied by a blonde girl.

She started and realized she'd been dozing. Her body was wet all over, her clothes stuck to her, she shivered.

A rumble that could hardly be heard startled her. People were standing for the gospel. She put her arms on the back of the pew ahead of her and rested her head on them. The oppression thought for her: if only I had never been.

And something else said: or could be little again, just little, and drink milk, and not know about cows. And again the images began, but this time she knew she was dreaming; and with a long effort as though she were pulling in the sea which had become cotton, she brought herself back to wakefulness.

"...were indignant; here is a man, they said, that entertains sinners, and eats with them. Where...."

In the distance, she could see the people standing, but she couldn't find the man who was talking. His voice travelled like sounds across a quiet lake, but it came from everywhere and seemed loud to her. Someone coughed and the voice was drowned out. The cough started off a flurry of others and some shuffling. She found the pulpit by another big pillar, it was hardly noticeable. Then the voice returned.

"...than over ninety-nine souls that are justified, and have no need of repentance. Or if some woman..."

A group of people walked past her, among them a young workman with steel-tipped heels. By the time the noise ended, the voice

48

had stopped and the silence of the mass was resumed.

She was fully awake now. Something had come at her from another angle, silently, without warning, something she always knew would return. She had entered a building to rest, and now she couldn't forget what building it was. Unwanted, a past drama whose resolution she thought she had determined a long time ago returned with new choices, and asked her to decide again. But this time there was too much to be undone. Why now, she sighed to herself, why must it come up now? I have nothing now, I'm empty. I can't even choose, I'm caught, I can't be anything but what I am now, right now. There's no choosing, there's no doing. All that's left is knowing. I know. I know that damnation is part of me. It's old, too old. I can only know. And wait for it to happen. Or... maybe not wait.

Footsteps distracted her. They came from the front, unhurried, and stopped. She thought they were next to her, but when she looked up she saw their owner in the next aisle along the wall. A young priest with an ugly face put on a light in the confessional and sat there reading.

She looked at him. And the idea of Meg
Latimer waiting made her leave the pew and
walk to the porch.

The steps to the cathedral were cracked and
under repair; workmen had left planks and
mortar troughs stacked to one side. Across the
wide frontage she saw a few people on the sidewalk and a few cars on the street. The sun was
climbing a little higher and made the tall downtown buildings look as if they were growing
into the light. The glare hurt her eyes. She had
her sunglasses out but she just held them. The
massiveness of the city frightened her, she was
upset at the thought of driving. You ought to
get back to Meg, her brain said, you're getting
jumpy. Meg will fix you up. Meg's the only one
who's any good for you now. You'd better take
those stairs before they start looking like cliffs
and the street backs up a thousand miles.
Meg'll bring you back to yourself. My self...A
bell rang three times inside the cathedral and
an old reflex started to bend her knees.

When she saw the speedometer needle point to
fifty, she stepped hard on the brake pedal. Tires
squealed and the car strained to keep in line.

Her hands were slippery on the wheel. She held on to the cross piece, doing twenty now, and struggled a kleenex out of her purse. She wiped her hands. It had never been this bad before. She had managed a regular pattern of dosage and usually knew how long she could stay away from the apartment or how much to take with her. But she preferred not to carry any; apart from the normal risks, some playful type might decide to tear up her purse.

She stopped for a light and felt relieved that she had seen it; the panic was passing, she put it all down to having seen Sandra. The light changed. Three blocks later she turned into Rotsley Avenue and stopped in front of the garage doors of number 88.

She opened the middle door and guided the long car through. As she slid the garage door shut, she felt her control returning. She checked her make-up and hair, glanced at her clothes; Meg mustn't see her agitated. She went through the metal fire-door into the corridor of the basement apartments.

A door opened. The way it opened, one turn of the knob which wasn't released, meant that no one was going to walk through it very quickly. She kept walking. But when she got to 1A, he stepped into the corridor. The snappy sports jacket didn't hide the fat. His shaved face was smiling but not confidently, and his head glistened under the thinning hair. He was all dressed up, looking ready to start out on a casual stroll, to share a fine day with the neighbors, to wave at buses as they passed.

"Hello, Miss Lucy," he said, but he couldn't make it sound right.

"Hello."

She tried to make that take her to the stairs.

"You look tired," he tried again. The sympathy suited him like jewellery suits a bull.

"I am tired," she said.

"Long drive?" His smile gained confidence.

She didn't answer.

"How about a drink before going upstairs?"

"No thanks, I'll just...."

"What difference does it make? It can't mean anything to you. I can treat you right." He was close to her now, the casual pose was gone. "It could do you a lot of good to be nice. A guy like me's in a position to make it tough for you otherwise."

She looked at him steadily, without hate. She knew he was defeated, and powerless, now that he had risked all in a banal threat. He was up against more than he realized. A word to Meg about this....

"Let's say you're a little drunk and leave it at that."

She walked past him and went up the stairs. He stood there burning in his righteous vanity.

As she reached the top of the flight, she became aware of the stairs; each one was a separate effort, not physically but mentally. Again, the feeling of unreality. Stairs. A hall. Doors to apartments. Worther fuming below and Meg waiting in No. 10. The individual decision, it seemed, for each step. She almost laughed. There was no turning back, so going ahead must be easy. But it wasn't. It wasn't really going ahead. It was like having to climb a ladder, downwards.

She put her key in No. 10 and walked in.

Meg Latimer was sitting at a bleached wood table with a scratch pad in front of her and a pencil in her hand. Elizabeth knew the routine: Meg didn't write anything, the pad was just for hasty calculations. She looked up as Elizabeth walked in and made a motion with her finger to indicate she wanted to finish what she was doing. Elizabeth crossed the room and sat down on the couch with a silent sigh. There was never much said when she or the others came back. Unless something had gone wrong, there was nothing to say. At other times, it was bright chatter about everything else, records, a few laughs, a few drinks, but this was rare enough; they didn't meet too often as a group and didn't exist for one another's benefit. This wasn't a home, or a club.

"You're late."

"They left around 6, the girls went first." There was no use lying to Meg Latimer; she had a way of knowing things, things like that.

"Then?"

"I drove around."

"Why didn't you come straight here?"

"I was tired. I wanted to get some air."

Meg lifted her cigarette from the ashtray and puffed at it. Her face was a little strained, the air of command was lost in nervousness. Elizabeth noticed that she was fully dressed and made up. This was unusual that early on a Sunday morning.

"You can get a lot of air in over an hour. It's eight, now."

"Well, I needed a lot of air, Meg."

Meg's eyes softened into normal hardness. She allowed herself a touch of sentiment toward this beautiful girl, she could enjoy her as one enjoys a beautiful animal, a small feeling that didn't interfere with things.

"They make trouble for you?"

"No, I was just tired. I sat on a bench and remembered when I was a little girl."

Now that danger to the girl, and to herself, was ruled out, Meg became angry. "I told you always to come here after. It's just smart, that's all. You might need an alibi, protection, anything. Some guy loses a wallet and thinks of you right away, or he gets an ache where it hurts and gets mad enough to go looking for you, or yells cop, and a day or two in the tank off the stuff'll make you say anything just to get a plain coke. Get it?"

"Yes, I get it. I don't know if I care."

Meg stood up and crushed out the cigarette clumsily. Her voice rose.

"To hell with that, I'll do the caring. Just you do as I say. Dot was picked up as a pickpocket, a pickpocket—the bastards—and now she's on file she's useless. Any guy with a lot of money to spend doesn't want to be bothered by cops.

And Sandra—gone, just gone. Hell, I wish I knew where that little bitch went to. She was big money. And you're big money, chicken, don't forget that."

Elizabeth stiffened inwardly at the name Sandra, she wondered if Meg knew; the suspicion dogged her until she realized she was too tired to judge right. Still, she thought that Meg was too shrill; almost upset. She nodded to Meg's words and said, "I have to get some sleep."

"There's something else." Meg's tone had changed, her nervousness was more apparent.

"What is it?"

"You'll have to go to the other apartment."

This had happened before, but Elizabeth had always been told in advance. She was going to ask a question, but the phone rang. Meg went to it quickly and spoke first.

"Yes?"

Then silence as she listened intently.

"Yes, now....I know it's later, but it couldn't be helped...."

She twirled the phone wire and held the receiver too tightly.

"Yes, right away....No."

She hung up.

"I'll get some clothes," Elizabeth said.

"No!" It was close to a scream. "Leave as you are."

"If it's only a delivery, I don't matter, Meg. Take it easy."

"It's not that, it's not that. Will you get going?"

She left and went quickly down the stairs not glancing at the front entrance. She made no noise going past Worther's door. Once in the garage she stopped to relax a little: whoever was coming had Meg scared and Meg wasn't the one to scare easily.

A blond-haired man in his thirties, almost chubby, in a summer suit and a sports shirt outside his trousers, was getting ready to close one of the outside garage doors. He was taking his time, and when he heard Elizabeth enter, he looked at her casually and smiled in a neighborly way. He wasn't a neighbor she had seen before.

"Would you leave it open?" she asked. "I'm on my way out."

"Sure," he said, and walked past her into the building.

A dark grey car that hadn't been there earlier was parked in such a way that she had to walk facing it to get to her own. She looked at it without interest and took out her keys. In the act of opening her door she realized with a start that almost turned her head around that there was someone in the back seat of the other car. Slowly she got behind the wheel and began backing out. With a passing glance as she moved away, she was able to make out a hat and sunglasses on an older man. She simply got the impression that he was an older man. He didn't move, but he seemed to be looking in her direction, looking steadily. A younger man would have betrayed his interest.

She backed out all the way to the street. Nothing happened.

On a Sunday morning, a man sits in the back seat of a car, in a garage, just a man sitting in a car, sitting there, watching calmly, as if he had no intention of getting out. Nobody'd notice on a Sunday morning, nobody would be in the garage...nobody except her, arriving accidentally. As she drove away she saw the garage door closing. And then she remembered there was a phone in the garage: they were on their way to see Meg.

The four rooms were sparsely furnished and kept undecorated beyond having curtains, a few pictures, and a rug. They weren't meant for gracious living, the success of looking like the advertisements, they were meant for living whose pain demanded fewer and fewer things: no radio, no television, no magazines, these she could get everywhere, a telephone known to very few, books of non-fiction to keep the brain engaged and distracted, a sewing machine and small racks for impossible embroidery; she had tried painting once, but the arts released the imagination too freely; she preferred the crafts, they were less self-centering.

This "other apartment" was a place Meg Latimer had allowed her to have, and it had developed into something like a home for her, a place unconnected with everything else where her unguarded moments wouldn't betray her. She didn't like living in one place, either one as busy as Latimer's or one as secluded and unknown as this, even if it was a refuge. It didn't solve anything, but at least it alternated pressures. In one, it was life that grew intolerable; in the other, it was her own self. And she juggled one against the other knowing that at one point the juggler's hand would tire.

She sat sideways on the couch and let her eyes look out the window. The apartment was on the fourth floor facing a park, and from where she was sitting the upper parts of the trees were visible and the sky beyond. A good view, if you wanted a good view, but this wasn't the right moment for that, it was just something in her range of vision. The room was quiet; from outside came the distant sounds of a few children in the park and muted traffic on the cross street. She wasn't sleepy. She had showered and changed and delayed till nine o'clock adhering grimly to the pattern she had set for the heroin. But no joy followed; she didn't go in for kicks, she was dealing with necessities. She felt grimly fortunate to be able to handle that necessity in a place of her own; she had long outgrown the group guilt of a "tea" party. Meg trusted her to use the apartment only as a home and with having on hand more than the dole she dispensed to the others. It was a sort of privilege, like a promotion that didn't bode well for the future. But Meg seemed to understand. They'd never fought over money, or the drug, or the work.

There had been fighting, but a strange kind: Meg fought, fought nothing, in rages like nightmares that exhausted her like sleepless nights. The violence and the suddenness of these had frightened Elizabeth at first; she expected the screaming and the abuse to be turned on her, to cut her off perhaps. But Meg's rages didn't affect her handling of things. They passed, and were never talked about. Elizabeth could always avoid them by coming here. Meg had been almost sympathetic about the apartment. She had checked it, of course; she checked everybody. She had an investment to protect, a little privacy to one of the girls didn't mean anything.

When Elizabeth noticed the sky and the unmoving trees getting warmer in the sun, she knew it was going to be a hot day and that she would have difficulty sleeping well. She could wait till nightfall when the green in the park cooled quickly and the wind blew through the rooms; but that meant trying to stay awake all day, dozing into half-real dreams and waking with starts to an unnatural day. She couldn't afford that: the thoughts she had demanded oblivion or complete alertness. In an in-between state, they would possess her and grow more insistent and stay in the mind like a frenzied cosmos excluding everything else and feeding on her own cerebral energy until mere exhaustion brought her back to the real world and the ever-present causes of it all. When breakdown comes, she thought, it will be something like that. But then they say some people attain a sort of peace that way: the exhausted juggler is no longer a juggler.

Nor is a dead one, she said to herself and laughed once. This is self-pity, a lot of sad words, who cares about dead jugglers? I'm not a juggler, I'm a....She stopped the debate before it ran away with her.

Three, slowly spaced, gentle knocks came from the door. She didn't get up, she knew who it was. A key was put into the lock, the door opened; it opened softly, apologetically, and a tall man with wide, soft eyes walked in. He walked in a self-consciously light-treading manner and closed the door as if it were made of eggshells. He was big, with wide shoulders and a heavy frame, but his air was totally diffident; he looked not quite fat, unexercised; the horn-rimmed glasses he wore suggested a prosperous public relations man, but his eyes and his deference belied that. Elizabeth felt no resentment at his arriving at that moment. The presence of another person assured a less dangerous depth of feeling.

"You don't have to knock, Jimmy," she said, "you know that." It was said kindly but wearily.

"I know, I know, but I don't want to startle you by walking in without warning. Did you just get up?"

"No, I came over about an hour ago. I haven't slept."

His face became pained at the implication and he turned to look at the chair near the bookcase before sitting in it.

"You look worried, Elizabeth."

His voice was pleasant, almost baritone; it dropped a little when he pronounced her name. He always called her that, and always softly.

"I'm...." She ached with the wish to talk about things, but the irony of that stopped her: she was the one who helped him and it couldn't be the other way around; he wasn't strong enough yet to reverse roles. She changed her statement to, "I'm tired, Jimmy, so tired I'm thinking strangely." Her life was as secret as her soul, she alone could know about Sandra, about her panic in the cathedral, about Meg's unpromising visitors, about her own inner wishes being formulated as a decision to have done with it all.

"Is there anything you want me to do?" he said. He knew too that service was easier to grant than support. He had no illusions, but he had more hope than she did, mainly because he had risen from a less profound depth and had had help, her help.

"Will you drive the car for me if I go out? I'm a little nervous."

"Of course. Do you...want me to go? I mean, now, do you want to be alone?"

"It doesn't matter," she said.

"Have you eaten anything? Had breakfast?"

"No, I haven't."

"I'll fix you something." He got up to go into the kitchen.

The phone rang. Jimmy knew it wasn't for him, only one person had Elizabeth's number from him, a psychiatrist he went to. They let it ring awhile. She knew it was Meg, unless Dr. Hildebrand....

"Hello," she said into the phone.

"It's me," said Meg's voice; she sounded cautious.

"Yes."

"Things have been happening. They saw you in the garage."

"I saw them. Who are they, Meg?"

"Let's say important people, chicken." Her voice had business in it now, sales talk articulation.

"Why are you calling?"

"There's something...special doing. You're to go."

"When?"

"I don't know. A few days, a week, maybe more. They'll let you know. In the meantime, you're...on vacation."

"Is there an out I can take? I don't like the sound of it." When she had said it, she realized how frightened she was.

"They told me," said Meg, "I told you. That's all there is to it. So long."

Elizabeth hung up and kept her hand on the receiver. Fear tried to define the future, to put shape on the huge nothingness of evil confronting her. She stared absorbedly at the warming day outlined by her window, and remained that way until sounds from another room reached her and almost enervated her with irony: bacon was frying in the kitchen.

3

THE PRESENT

In daylight, the Hillton Road apartments showed their size but looked less dressed up without the gush of light from the wide entrance; the glass-wall front mirrored the street and could have passed for a store; but there were no stores in this neighborhood. Henderson drove past the building, parked on the cross street, and began walking back. It was a little after ten, and already the July heat made him walk slowly.

The street was quiet, summer quiet: a few birds chirping sharply dominated the sounds of distant traffic; a laundry van passed Henderson and made its way down the slope and behind the apartment building; a chauffeur waited, not daring to lounge, by a black car; further up the street where the real estate consisted of big homes, a milkman hurried up and down the long walks racing the noon sun; a clothesline pulley squeaked from nowhere; a group of sun-darkened gardeners in an open 1/2-ton truck smiled as they passed; Henderson waved idly, and tried to see if any of the parked cars down the street had an occupant. A nice, sunshiny morning, slow-moving and peaceful after a summer night's rain. They had washed the sidewalk where she had fallen, some of it had been scraped clean; Henderson looked at it without stopping and went into the building.

The last label on the buzzer panel had only "penthouse" printed on it. He pressed the button and waited, looking through the glass wall and doors that separated him from the elevator and the stairs. He had phoned Mr. Keerson with the number the phone company had supplied, but Mr. Keerson had been out. He was still out.

As he waited, the elevator light came on, and eventually a tall man with waved grey hair came out and walked fussily to the lobby doors.

"Lovely morning, lovely," said the man singingly.

"Yes, it certainly is," said Henderson just to say something.

"I suppose you've heard about last night?"

"No," said Henderson casually.

"Seems somebody had a girl." He winked and smiled and rubbed his hands and giggled as though remembering stag party pictures.

"Oh."

"Yes, the police came, you know."

"Is that right?"

"Somebody must have reported them, maybe they were making too much noise." The man burst into a giggly laugh before he could finish.

"Did they catch them?" said Henderson.

"I don't know. I'll get the rest of it later. Well, I must be running along. Good-bye."

He left, still gurgling, and got into a waiting cab.

Henderson rang the manager's apartment

and went in to see him. After some haggling and a promise to fix things if Mr. Keerson complained, he was given the key. He rode the elevator up, rang several times, and let himself in.

Nobody seemed to be home, and nothing seemed to have been disturbed. In the living room, the drapes were still pulled open, the air-conditioning was off, and Mr. di Callitiere's huge table still occupied its place of honor. Henderson went over the room carefully, and then starting at the front door he went towards the terrace examining the wall-to-wall carpeting, looking for anything that might be there, a key that may have let her in and that she may have dropped or thrown away. But there was nothing. Again from the front door, he turned into the nearest room on his right, a bedroom that also led to the terrace. With the idea that she may have changed her clothes in the penthouse, he searched the closets, the dressers, but all these were empty. Further off in the main hall, he found another bedroom, and in that were a man's clothes and furnishings but nothing to indicate her presence. He examined the dining-room, the bathroom, the hall closets, a room with nothing in it at all, and finally the kitchen where he sat down at the table and stared at the refrigerator.

The place was too clean, too unlived-in. It had an air of inactivity, a spurious innocence that almost managed to make unreal the patch of washed sidewalk below and the body in the morgue. A cover-up had been made, but it could have been made by her: a suicide who didn't want others to know. Could be, anything could be. But the kind of deliberation needed for that pointed to someone else, someone who tidied up too well. Henderson knew he had very little to go on. He took out a cigarette, thought better of it, and stood up to go.

Just then, the doorbell chimed.

With a start, he went to the kitchen door. The bell chimed again. He looked out into the hall at the front door and waited. A key was fitted into the lock, turned dully, and the door opened. Henderson moved back into the kitchen.

The person's footsteps were soft thuds on the carpeting, rapid and cautious, sounding like a man's. They came in Henderson's direction, stopped briefly, and died away as the person seemed to go into the next room. It was the room that contained a man's furnishings.

Henderson eased himself into the hall and froze as he heard the snap-cluck sounds of a suitcase being opened. A dresser drawer was opened and closed, another was pulled open and left open. Henderson edged forward and finally stood sideways in the doorway.

A man with thinning curly hair and wearing an ordinary-looking brown suit was putting things in a large suitcase. He was moving quickly. From the dresser he had taken only certain shirts and a small automatic pistol. He was now taking suits out of the closet. He felt for one in particular, seemed satisfied that it contained what he was feeling for, folded it and dropped it in the suitcase. He took the other suits indiscriminately and threw them in until it was filled. Without stopping, he looked for and found a travelling bag and continued with his work.

When he was finished, he picked up the suitcases, turned and saw Henderson.

"Just keep holding on to those," said Henderson as he walked up to the man.

"Who the f... are you?" the man blurted in surprise. Henderson removed a revolver from inside the man's coat and stepped back.

"Those aren't yours," he ventured, indicating the suitcases, "you don't live here."

"Neither do you, brother," the man said, angry but careful.

"Put them down and tell me what you're doing here."

"The hell with you. I'm here legit. You tell me."

Henderson told him and showed him the badge.

"Cops," the man said, "cops, there was nothing said about cops." He put down the suitcases and looked puzzled.

"Who are you?" asked Henderson.

"My name's Maet, Charley Maet."

"What are you doing here?"

"Guy asked me to pick up his stuff."

"Who is he?"

"A guy."

"Don't get cute, Charley. I could find out by checking these clothes, and I could take you in for breaking and entering."

"Hell," he shouted, "breaking! I had a key. And the guy that lives here *asked* me to come and get his stuff. That's all there is to it."

"For this you need a gun."

"I got a permit. I run a car business. I've been

robbed before. Look, you got nothing on me; I'm going."

"This could make a lot of trouble for you, Charley. It might make you an accessory to a killing."

"I don't know anything about that."

"You'll have to show me, Charley."

The man sat on the bed, confused, and he thought it over.

"All right," he said.

"Who's the guy?"

"Herby Lefram. He works for this guy, Keerson." He indicated the suite.

"What kind of work?"

"I dunno."

"Who's Keerson?"

"I dunno, some big shot."

"How do you know I'm not Keerson?"

"Herby said he wouldn't be here, said he was a dark-haired guy. You're getting grey."

"When did Lefram contact you?"

"Last night, about 1:30. I was home. He called, said he was downtown and needed a car, not a new one or a loud one, but good. So I got one and drove it to him."

"What's the make?"

"52 Ols, dark blue."

"Licence."

"I'll have to look it up for you."

"Where did you bring the car?"

"Downtown. Then he told me to come up here today and get his stuff. He gave me the keys. Said I was to hold everything till I heard from him. And that's all. I took a cab home."

"What does Lefram look like?"

"Blond guy, not fat, but fat-looking, round face. Average height, good dresser."

"Where was he going?"

"He didn't say."

"Where did he phone you from?"

"A place called the Evening Star, it's on Rotsley. I met him in the next block. Boy, did he look beat."

"OK, Charley, when he reaches you, you call me, eh?"

"Are you kiddin'? Herby's no lily. I want to keep living."

Henderson didn't press it any further; he took phone numbers and addresses from Maet and left him. On the way to Rotsley Avenue he stopped to phone in the information and to have the man watched. It seemed like a waste of the city's time, but it looked as if Herby

Lefram had seen things; he may even have done things.

The Evening Star Café had a neon sign and a canopy that covered the half dozen steps to the porch; the entrance was a natural color plywood door, and the whole place had the typical look of a night-spot converted from an old-fashioned house: a look that tried hard to be cosy, and only succeeded in looking half painted. It was a little early for it to be doing business, and Henderson waited to see if anyone was around.

She had a swizzle-stick from this place. A bar near home to drop into for a quiet drink. A place where people knew you, but didn't know anything about you. Here she could pass as a model, an artist, an actress, a student, anything compatible with a mild taste for night life. It wasn't a contact place for pushers, or it would be known; she didn't do business from here, or that too would be known. Just a nice quiet barful of fake friends. A place neither high nor low, a middle-class underworld, full of night people, fake intellectuals, big-time posers, one-flash celebrities, literate failures, world-changers who wait and watch the bottle go down, and young wits and newly sophisticated girls who feel they are wanted and liked by people who are indifferent to anything except money. A nice quiet bar. He laughed. There's no such thing; there's only a few quiet hours when the people haven't come back yet.

He got out of the car and walked into the club.

The lobby was empty. A checkroom that looked more like a broom closet was crowded under a stairway, and two phone booths almost hid one wall; past these an archway led to the bar. A radio was on; the announcer was trying to get a housewife to answer a simple question; the beep that indicates a recorded phone call added an air of urgency to the proceeding. There was no one listening to it. The place was large for a converted house; the tables were small and closely spaced; near the street-windows was a piano on a step-up platform.

He sat at the bar and listened to the announcer's professional cheerfulness. Radios never get tired. After a while a man in a white shirt with no tie and rolled up sleeves came in behind the bar carrying a box. He put it under the counter and looked at Henderson unpleasantly.

"Nothing," said Henderson. "I just want to

ask a few questions."

"Is that right? About what?"

Henderson took the picture of the girl and placed it on the top of the bar so the man could see it.

"This girl. Know her?"

The man's face hardened, his eyes narrowed a little; suspicion was growing into certainty.

"Who's asking?" he muttered.

"I am."

"And who the hell does that make you?"

Henderson told him, and continued, "Do you know this girl?"

"Some."

"She come in here often?"

"Once a week, maybe less."

"Alone?"

"Sometimes alone, sometimes with a guy."

"Same guy every time?"

"Yeah."

"What does this guy look like?"

"Tall, with glasses."

"How old?"

"Thirty-five maybe."

"When was the last time she was in here?"

"I dunno. Ask the night man."

"When's he going to be in?"

"At night."

"Look," said Henderson, "why don't you just tell it? I can get it from anybody who works here. It might as well be you."

"That's all there is. She comes in here. Just another customer."

"This girl would not be just another customer. She'd attract attention. More guys than one would be up here asking you about her."

"So l don't know."

"Where can I find the boss?"

"In the back."

Henderson crossed the bar and went through two swing-doors into a short corridor. A door marked "Office" was open all the way. He walked in and saw a well-dressed plump man with a sporty face sitting at a desk covered with papers and magazines and glass stains. The man stood up and said in a loud voice, "Yes, what can I do for you?" He emphasized the "you." Henderson showed him the badge, the picture, and explained what he wanted.

"Never here," said the man, "I'm never here. See my barman."

"I did. He didn't say much."

"Well, I can't help that. Maybe if you tried another day."

"Don't you run this place?"

"Run it? No. I own it. Couldn't run it. That girl. A real looker. Maybe she sings?"

"No."

"Well, if that girl wants a job, send her in to me, ask for Matty, I got other places...."

"Yeah."

Henderson went back to the bar. Somebody was howling a song on the radio, but again there was nobody listening to it. He went out and drove up the street to number 88 where she had lived.

Nobody was in at Latimer's, at least nobody was answering the door. He kept ringing, supposing vaguely that she was a late sleeper. But he almost smiled at the idea: after having placed a blond chubby lad called Lefram in the vicinity, he was sure Mrs. Latimer wouldn't want to be questioned about last night. Still he had only a few coincidences, not yet connected by any real testimony or honest admissions. All he had was a few facts, but he knew that facts get made by people; and he was getting around to seeing the people. A hard-bitten operator like Latimer would know where her girls went, she'd send them, she'd know who was there, and in general what went on. Maybe this morning she'd feel like telling some of it: how perhaps the party got a little foggy and people thought they could fly, or that others could.

The tinny gaiety of a radio down the hall boomed in a muffled way as a loud record came on. Enough time had passed. He let himself in with Elizabeth Lucy's keys.

For a moment there was complete silence. The radio in the hall couldn't be heard. No one snored, or shouted, or patted in on slippers. It was broken as a car passed outside. The window was open a little, he could tell from the clarity of the sound, but the venetian blinds were closed. The living room was more or less as he remembered it, but in subdued daylight the whole tone was different. It was when he had adjusted to it that he noticed that two table lamps were on. It didn't seem to mean anything, and he couldn't tell how long they'd been on. But he was beginning to feel that Mrs. Latimer had pulled out in a hurry last night.

He left the living room and looked into what

had been the girl's room. He checked the closet and a few dresser drawers: her things were still there. The two other bedrooms had the typical look of rooms used just to sleep in: clothes strewn over chairs and the unmade beds, towels on the floor, cosmetics and kleenex all over the dressers, newspapers and magazines where they had been tossed, unemptied ashtrays, and glass stains on the end tables: the general chaos of living. He walked through it with deliberate indifference and made his way down the hall into the kitchen.

The sink and the counter were stacked with dirty dishes, no large plates he noticed, just side plates, cups and saucers, cutlery, glasses; they probably ate out and left this for the cleaning woman. There were more dishes on the table, all used, napkins, remnants of sandwiches, cigarette butts in the cups. Some of the cupboard doors were open revealing lightly stacked shelves. The refrigerator didn't have much food in it. A frying pan with hardened fat in it was on the electric stove. On the floor next to the stove was a garbage container, its overflow stuffed into large paper bags. In one corner was an automatic washing machine; he noticed that the dial was at "Off" in the section indicating a fabric cycle: that made sense, he couldn't imagine Mrs. Latimer doing washing for the girls. He let the idea pass, he was learning nothing new hanging around in a dirty kitchen.

For four people who may or may not be home and who ate out, they certainly made a lot of garbage. The foot-operated can was full, an open paper bag was close to full, and another was closed and tied with string. It didn't stink, so that it hadn't lain here that long. He found a newspaper and spread it on the floor. With a meat knife he saw lying in the sink, he cut the string of the third garbage bag and touching it as little as possible he turned it over. Refuse consisting of odds-and-ends of food, ashes and cigarette butts, paper and other unidentifiable things fell out; the rest stuck a little; with a slight flip, the bag yielded clothes.

Using the knife on the blunt side, he hooked a strap and gingerly drew out a slip which he shook and placed on a kitchen chair. He continued this till he had placed on the chair the slip, a pair of white gloves, a bra, panties, and a pale green dress; it may have been close-fitting. Latimer had said the Lucy girl left here wearing this the night before.

Careless, damned careless, he thought, standing with his hands held out in front of him as though they were wet. Maybe not careless, maybe Latimer planned to be back before this, maybe the cleaning woman who would throw this stuff out is late or not coming, and maybe the dress means nothing at all, maybe Latimer hates to be reminded of the dear departed, maybe a lot of things. He ran the water in the sink and washed his hands, wiping them on a dishtowel. He left the kitchen and took the hall on his way to the living room where the phone was.

He had missed it coming from the other direction but now he was able to see it clearly: the bathroom door was ajar and the light was on. He went to it. It opened about half way and stopped. He didn't push, he didn't want to disturb anything; he was able to sidle in easily. Mrs. Latimer hadn't left in a hurry last night, she stayed home and died.

She was dressed as he had last seen her, now lying on her side with legs crossed as though walking grotesquely; her face was turned to the floor, partly entangled in the bathroom rug, and her hands and arms were curled like folded wings. Examining the floor before stepping on it, he straddled the body and looked around it. Bits of shattered glass were reflected in the light, and near her feet, beside the bathtub, he saw pieces of what must have composed a hypodermic needle. He straightened up and took his former position near the door. The medicine cabinet was open, but it was filled with too many supplies to warrant a search now. He sidled out again and went to the living room.

He called in for a lab crew, and called Cerini at home.

In less than an hour, the apartment was crowded: two men from the laboratory division, a coroner who looked as if he resented being dragged from a better practice, a fingerprint man who held everything up before they could take the bathroom door down to work inside, two other men from the narcotics division, and a silent no-nonsense observer brought in for the RCMP. Henderson and Cerini waited until the coroner finally committed himself to a tentative guess that Meg Latimer had died of poison, probably cyanide, which could have been self-administered, perhaps some five to ten hours ago. On the surface, it offered a chance to wrap things up: Meg Latimer killed or saw the girl die, and, upset or guilty, she took her own life.

But below the surface, Henderson saw only the improbability of two suicide-looking deaths: the Lucy girl, maybe; but not an old-time operator like Meg Latimer.

While the work continued, Henderson and Cerini went downstairs to apartment 1A. Worther came to the door carrying a napkin; and this time he was dressed for sport in beltless slacks and matching shirt, all beige with brown trimmings, with a face shaved and sweet-smelling, and as full of confidence as a card sharp at a parish bridge.

"Oh, you guys," he said on seeing them. "What is it now? I'm having lunch."

"Just a few more questions," said Henderson.

"Didn't you find your party?"

"Yeah, we found her," said Cerini.

"Well?"

"Let's go inside," said Henderson.

They went in and remained standing in the living room. Worther said, "I got toast goin'," and went into the kitchen and came back shutting the door behind him.

"Last night," said Henderson, "you said you didn't see Elizabeth Lucy leave the building."

"That's right, I didn't."

"You just took it for granted she was out,

eh?" said Cerini.

"Yeah, I did. I coulda been wrong. Was I wrong?"

"When we left here," continued Henderson, ignoring the question, "did you see anyone around?"

"No...."

"You're sure?"

"Yeah, I'm sure. I went to bed."

"You didn't leave your apartment?"

"I was in bed. I don't sleepwalk."

"Did you see Mrs. Latimer any time after we left?"

"No."

"You didn't see any of her girls coming back?"

"Whatta you mean, her girls...?"

"Stuff it, Worther," Cerini rasped at him, "nobody could operate from this building without you knowing it. Did you see anybody that belongs to the Latimer apartment?"

Somebody coughed in the kitchen. Worther began talking loudly about how they were pushing him around. Henderson strolled into the kitchen. "What's the big idea?..." came Worther's voice behind him. He closed the door.

The girl was somewhere in her twenties, good-looking in a dull sexy way, made up and wearing a kimono halfheartedly. She was sitting at the table eating boiled eggs and sipping coffee.

"Brunch," she said. "What's all the noise about in there? You a tenant?"

"Why a tenant?"

"He's always yapping with the tenants. Who are you?"

"Just a guy. You Mrs. Worther?"

That sent her into gales of laughter.

"That's a real good one," she said, and added more seriously, "I'm Mrs. Nobody."

"Just a friend of Worther's, eh?" He sat down opposite her.

"Not even that, dad," she said through the coffee, "not even that."

"What's your name?"

"Sue."

"Is that all?"

"For talking purposes, you don't need much more, do you?"

"You live in apartment 10, eh? With Mrs. Latimer?"

"So? I gotta live somewhere."

"How come you're down here with Worther?"

She laughed again as though he had asked her what a bathroom was for.

"You're asking a lot of questions, dad, what's the score on this?"

"We're doing fine just like this."

"Not any more, I smell something."

"My name's Henderson," he said and showed his badge.

She thought things over for a while and said, "Look, I'm not gonna talk myself into a jam."

"You won't. Just listen to the questions and you'll see."

"All right," she said reluctantly, and before he could speak she inserted, "You after Worther?"

"No, not directly. What time did you come home last night?"

"You after...Meg, Mrs. Latimer?"

"No. Answer my question."

"I got in after three. Maybe closer to 3:30."

"Mrs. Latimer was in?"

"Yeah, she was in. So was that slob in there."

"Worther?"

"Him."

"In where, here or upstairs?"

"Upstairs at Meg's. Then he went out. And I was told to come down here."

"Told by Mrs. Latimer."

"That's right. Look if it's her you're....."

"I said it wasn't. He was here when you got here?"

"I'll say he was. This is the first time he's even got close."

"What time was it?"

"Exactly twenty-five to four. I told Meg as much, sending me out at that hour."

"Did you or he leave the apartment after that?"

"Nope."

"Was there anybody else in Mrs. Latimer's apartment?"

"No."

"You're sure?"

"No, I'm not sure. I wasn't there long enough to see anybody."

"Does Meg use a hypo?"

Her eyes went wide at the question.

"Why?"

"Does she?"

"Yeah, she does. But why are you asking?"

"Meg's dead, with a hypo," he said, and continued over her exclamations, "you'll have to come downtown...."

"No."

"...just to say what you've said to me and maybe a little more about Meg." She was getting panicky and he omitted any reference to the Lucy girl. "If you're on the stuff, Sue, play along with us, because that way you can look for a cure on the outside." She shook her head yes. "Come on, you get dressed and stay in the bedroom till it's time to go."

The girl ran across the living room not looking at Worther who sat glumly in an armchair.

"Sue, from Latimer's, he was up there last night," Henderson summarized for Cerini and turned to Worther. "Let's have all of it, all of it."

"So I got me a dame in here. Hell, a guy's human...."

"From Latimer's."

"Sure, from Latimer's; that's what they're for."

"Way out of your class, Worther," said Cerini.

"Up to now all you've been doing was sneaking a look."

"So I had the price."

"You mean, you had something on Meg

Latimer," Henderson said. "You waited till you had a real chance, last night was it, you couldn't keep your hands off it."

"Neither could you if you had classy broads like that walkin' past your door every day."

"And night," said Cerini.

"Yeah, yeah, and night. To hell with you. I'm not talking."

Henderson lit a cigarette and sat down. Cerini walked over to Worther and stood in front of him.

"Look," he said, "you may be thinking you'll stay in good with these broads if you keep your trap shut. The party's over, Worther. Reason one: Meg Latimer is dead...."

"Holy....," said Worther and cursed out his surprise.

"...Reason two: that girl in there might, just might, be your alibi. And if you think you can build a little love nest here, she's liable to get sore enough to forget she was here."

Cerini walked away to let him think it over and after a while he spoke.

"When you guys came here last night asking about the Lucy dame, I knew something was up, so when you left I went up there and put the proposition to Meg Latimer. She didn't tell me anything, she just said she'd fix me up."

"What about the Lucy girl's actions last night?"

"Well, about 11:30 she left with Meg Latimer. I happened to hear the lobby door bang shut, so I looked out the window there and saw the two of them get into her car."

"Whose car?" asked Henderson.

"The Lucy girl's."

"How was she dressed?"

"Dressed? Hell, I wouldn't know, she was wearing a dress, that's all there is to it."

"A plain dress?"

"I suppose so."

"Nothing fancy like an evening dress?"

"No, no, nothing like that, just a dress."

"What color was it?"

"I dunno, green maybe, maybe blue, I couldn't tell ya."

"Was she carrying anything, a box, a suit-case, something like that?"

"I dunno."

"Was Latimer carrying anything?"

"I wasn't looking at her."

"All right, go on."

"I stayed up looking at the late show, and about half past one I hear a car screeching into the driveway, in a hurry like, so I get ready to take a look when I hear the garage door rumble. Meg Latimer and this guy come busting out of the garage real fast, she goes upstairs and he goes out the front door. That's all I seen. Then the late show ended, I turned on the radio and had a few beers. Then you guys came in."

"What did this guy look like?"

"Lessee, I just got a look at the back of him. He was not too big, looked well-dressed, sporty like, yeah and he had light hair, blond like."

"He didn't see you?"

"No."

"Maybe you're lucky, for such a busy man."

A short pouty-looking girl in a glistening dress was singing in an advanced way, "I don't want lovin'—that just passes the time of day, I want—lovin' that means...."

It was nine that night, and the Evening Star Café was slowly stirring into life; the song sounded like a rehearsal, but by midnight somebody would believe in it. The place looked well filled in the dim light, and was perhaps at half capacity: a group of tourists taking in the local night-life; a few clusters of young people looking used to the big time; a noisy jazz argument at one table, loud voices raised in contradiction; along the wall a party of six, crisply dressed; ill at ease with drinks; the general background of people, bottles, talk; the odd quiet table, here and there a grim couple, a silent man drinking alone.

Henderson and Cerini made their way to the bar. The three men talking earnestly at the other end didn't notice them; a girl approached to order something and changed her mind when Cerini looked at her casually. The barman came over.

"Yes, sir," he said with a cheerful abruptness.

Henderson showed his identification. "We'd like to ask you a few things."

"You the one was in this morning?"

"That's right." He took out the girl's picture. "The other barman said she comes here off and on."

"She does."

"With somebody?"

"Yeah, but I wouldn't know who. A girl like that, you don't look at the guy. Anyway most of the time she's alone. Once with a nice young kid, a real looker, she couldn't have been out of her teens."

"You noticed?" said Cerini.

"Yeah, mister, I noticed. I got kids of my own. This girl," he tapped the picture on the bar, "is in the rackets, so the talk goes."

"Yeah, we've heard. Was she in last night?" asked Cerini.

"Yeah, she was, about this time, maybe a little later, maybe nine-thirty."

"Alone?"

"Alone."

"How long did she stay?"

"An hour, maybe less."

"How was she dressed?"

"I couldn't say for sure. No, I don't really know."

"Something else," said Henderson, "later on, about 1:30, did a blond chubby guy come in here?"

"1:30, eh? Wouldn't be very crowded then. A bunch of young guys were pooling their cash...and then I was...yeah, I remember, I was deciding to clean up, yeah, and this guy asks for some Wiser's, a double. He could've been blond."

"Would you know him if you saw him again?"

"Maybe, only maybe. If he came in and I said: weren't you in here last night, and he said yeah, then I'd know."

"He won't be in. Can you tell us anything more about the girl?"

"No, but maybe Gregory can."

"Gregory?"

"He works here, he sometimes waits on the girl. In slack times, they talk a little."

"Where is he?"

"He's in the washroom."

"Will he come out this way?"

"Not for a while. He works in there."

Henderson left Cerini with the barman and walked across the room dodging chairs to the door marked "men." Behind it was a short passage, another sign "toilet" with an arrow pointing downwards, and stairs going below. He went down and finally entered a large washroom, well-kept, and boasting of several hand-drying gadgets and a shoeshine chair. A tall angular man was washing his hands and craning his neck in the mirror trying to decide if he needed a shave. An old Negro sat in an armchair with a whisk in one hand, a magazine in the other. Henderson went to a urinal.

"I might need a shave later," the tall man said drying his hands, "can you fix me up?"

"Not officially," said the old Negro, "but I might find an electric razor somewhere."

The man nodded and gave him a bill and left.

Henderson went over to the old Negro.

"Are you the man they call Gregory?"

"That's right," he said in a serious tone. "You're a detective."

"Yes." He took out the picture. "Maybe you could tell me a few things about this girl."

The old man took the picture and looked at it. Nothing in his ridged face said he recognized her.

"I don't know very many girls, Mr...."

"Henderson."

"...Mr. Henderson. Down here..."

"I was told you might know her a little."

"You can be told a lot of things, mister, telling's easy."

"That's why I check where I can."

The old man went back to the picture.

"This girl," he said, "is she in trouble?"

"Not any more," said Henderson, "she's dead."

The stairs rumbled beyond the door, voices sounded, and two men came in talking; they fell silent when they saw Henderson. The old man kept looking at the picture until they went out again.

"She was here last night," the old man stated in a flat tone, "she sat alone near the wall away from the piano. I served her coffee. She said hello to me but we didn't talk, there were too many customers. She had on a green dress, like she was going out. But that doesn't mean anything, she was always well dressed. She's dead, eh? Hard to believe."

"Nobody spoke to her, picked her up?"

"Not that I know of. And she was no pickup. I know what she was. Maybe it's better that she died now. Years from now....Anyway, she left about ten-thirty. I just noticed she was gone and went over to collect the cup: she hadn't taken much of the coffee, and she let a cigarette burn down in the ashtray."

"You liked her, eh?"

"We talked. Two human beings. We talked. That's all, but that's a lot."

"Anything I should know about?"

"No, no information, just human talk."

"I'm also checking about a blond guy that came in here about half past one last night."

"Just drinking?"

"He had one at the bar, but he might've made a phone call."

"That's right, he did. He barked at me in the lobby for where the phone was. That was all."

"Ever see him before?"

"No."

"The two barmen said the girl used to come in with a tall guy with glasses. Ever see him?"

"A few times."

"Do you know who he is?"

"I think she called him Jimmy once."

"Do you know where I can find him?"

"He was here earlier. Maybe he's gone up the street to her place."

"OK, thanks."

"You gonna tell me how she died?"

He told him. Then he left to join Cerini at the bar.

The place seemed a little more crowded; the singer was sitting with a group of people and the piano player was providing background to the general swirl of talk and noise. Cerini had half a glass of ginger ale in front of him; he listened to Henderson's brief summary of the talk with the old Negro and said, "By the wall, just behind us, a tall lad, glasses, could be him.

Came in when you were downstairs." Henderson looked at him in the mirror.

He was in a sports shirt, looking big in a gentle way, and a little lost, staring at his drink, and then glancing at any movement near the lobby. Cerini made his way to the washroom. In a short while, the old Negro came out, picked up a tray at the bar and went around to a few tables. When he came to the man with glasses, he was addressed, said something in reply, continued to other tables, and finally came back to the bar where he simply nodded yes.

Henderson went over to the man's table and sat down as he said, "If you're a guy called Jimmy, I want to talk to you."

"Oh," said the man, "about what?"

"I understand you know a girl called Elizabeth Lucy."

"Yes, that's correct, but until you explain we're not going to have much of a conversation."

He had the tone and precision of a well-educated man; but his manner was almost shy in contrast to the definiteness of his words.

Henderson said, "You haven't heard then."

"What haven't I heard?"

Cerini had come out of the washroom and

was at the table. He sat down and Henderson explained who they were.

"I'm Jim Rande," he said politely. "Now what is it that I haven't heard?"

"When was the last time you saw the Lucy girl?" asked Henderson.

"Something's happened to her," he exclaimed looking uncertainly from Henderson to Cerini. His eyes were growing wide with panic or fearful concern, Henderson couldn't tell which, but he knew that this man was going to react hard to what he was going to be told. Cerini opened with, "Drink up, we'll tell you in good time."

"Tell me, tell me, for God's sake let's start at the right end."

"Something did happen," said Henderson quietly, "she's dead."

Jimmy Rande's face simply went stony and he stared without expression at the lobby. He stayed that way for what seemed a long time, opening his mouth to speak words he didn't utter, until he found voice enough to say, "Tell me about it."

Henderson told him the essentials of her death and no more; the man's reactions were open enough, but in Henderson's experience any sort of reaction was compatible with any sort of innocence or guilt. He ended with, "She really hasn't been identified by anybody yet."

"Didn't Meg Latimer...? No, of course not, she wouldn't."

"When did you last see the Lucy girl?"

"I...yes, I suppose you do have to ask all these questions. It seems so...so...it doesn't feel right to talk about her so objectively. I last saw her at the apartment last night after dinner; that is, she was there when I arrived after dinner."

"The apartment, up here on this street?"

"No, another one. It's not far from here. She left about eight-thirty or nine to go to Latimer's."

"This other apartment, is it one of Latimer's places?"

"One of...? Oh no, it was Elizabeth's, a place where she could be away from Latimer and her...doings."

"She didn't get along with Latimer, is that it?"

"No, there was no difficulty that way. Elizabeth...got along, she needed...I can't express it. She knew exactly what she was, how stuck she was in that whole mess, and she needed a place where she could be alone to work things out, or just keep thinking them out, just keep thinking...."

He stopped talking and finished his drink

and strained to keep his face from moving. His eyes were wet.

Henderson said, "I'd like to see that apartment, there may be something."

They stood up and went out of the Evening Star, Cerini walking behind in a necessary and official mistrust. In the car, Jimmy said, "I'll identify her."

"It's Elizabeth."

He looked, and then tears overcame his face and he wept openly, wept without apology to the two men who stood by not unmoved. He said, "I'm all right, I'm all right," to indicate he wasn't breaking down, "it's just her like this. She couldn't see a way out. She thought she couldn't die well." He made no effort to hide his emotion, and Henderson, who had to judge, thought it was genuine.

They led him out to the car and began the silent drive to the other apartment. The only time he spoke was to give them the address.

In the lobby and at the apartment door, Henderson fitted the remaining two of the four keys that had been in her handbag. Jimmy led the way inside, turned on lights, offered drinks which were declined, and mixed one for himself.

"Do you live here?" asked Henderson.

"Yes, I do, in a way. At least I have no other place. It's a long story."

"Did you live with her?"

"No," he said, "no, nothing like that. That...just wasn't possible."

"Was she in love with you?"

"No. It wasn't...I can't talk about it now."

Henderson had little trouble checking the orderly and sparsely furnished rooms. Except for books, a certain taste in arrangement and color, the clothes, the known facts, there seemed to be a strict anonymity to the place, no documents except a lease; there should have been a bankbook, he felt, or car insurance, or a bill for clothes: Latimer could have had them, of course, but disposed of them. In a first-aid kit he found small capsules of heroin looking as normal as aspirin, not really hidden away, yet not obvious. He took it with him back into the living room where Cerini and Jimmy sat without speaking.

Jimmy was sitting sideways in an armchair looking at the screened open window beyond which was nothing but the hot night. He was drinking his second drink.

"I disgraced my family in college," he said tonelessly, "and they cut me off, the other fellow's family cared less so he was luckier, but I drifted into that strange netherworld where types like me go, and it got worse, and my mind got worse, and I went real low. It was at that point that I met Elizabeth, an accident, the way life is an accident. I was in a place, a fancy place north just out of town, you probably know it, where anybody can go, anybody, and I was with somebody I was involved with, and he picked that time for what he thought was funny but what to me was persecution: the whole place was having a hell of a wicked time at my expense, and this didn't go down too well with me because then I was only a few months away from a breakdown I'd had, and things exploded inside, disproportionately of course, it's always like that, isn't it?—and I ran out of the place. It was like running out of hell.

"She'd been there with some fellow from out of town who wanted to see the wicked spots; he wasn't too fit, was overdoing it, anyway he had to leave, and she didn't go with him because he had called off the night. So she was in the place alone and didn't have to worry about trouble from the fellow that left; he was a considerate type and had paid Meg and wouldn't complain later. So she saw the whole business happening to me, running out and all. I was panicky, I couldn't even see where I was going. Without knowing it I ran into the parking lot and sat down on the asphalt between the building and a car, it was her car, but I didn't know it. I sat there and cried and waited for it to pass, afraid it might stay and be another breakdown. It seems silly, doesn't it?—but when it's on you, that's the way it is, I felt like a kid, small, physically helpless, existing inexorably but always more weakly than the things around it—oh, it's just like that, like that.

"Anyway, she came out after a while and found me there, she wasn't surprised, just attentive, she takes things that way, she doesn't seem to get caught off guard, she just accepts what's there. It took me some time to realize she was there. I looked up at her and said, I'll go in a minute, this is your car, eh?' She said it was and asked me where I was going, and I said home, and then said nowhere because home had been with that type that was bugging me. Then she said, 'You can't just drift, the

police'll take you in.' I said I didn't care, and
then I remembered the institution I'd been in
three months before, and how maybe I'd be
sent to another to straighten me out, the psychiatrists couldn't do a thing. I broke into crying
again, this time really ashamed that I was doing
so in front of her. I kept saying 'I'm sorry, I'm
sorry, it just won't stop, I'm sorry.' She didn't
say anything, she opened the car, and helped
me up, and got me inside. We came here.

"She made coffee and we sat in the kitchen
drinking it. She hadn't said a word all this time.
She didn't speak until I did. When I told her
things, and said I had a doctor who looks after
me, part of the family deal, and the whole
bloody history of it, she called him and he came
over and they talked when I was asleep under
sedation. And the next day, she told me I could
use this place for a home, as I liked, with one
condition, no one was to know about it, no one
was to come up, no one was to see me if she
came with anyone through a circumstance she
couldn't avoid. It was a place for me to use alone
when things got bad, or good, it didn't matter.

"She was taking an awful chance as I found
out later, because she really needed this place,

and the game she was in was tricky. A weak guy like me around could have ruined everything, even had her killed. And all that should have happened, it was all in the cards, the unbreakable pattern of the world I was in. But it didn't happen, it just didn't happen, I wasn't noble or even grateful really then, but it just didn't happen.

"I got to know her, bit by bit, and the more I got to know her and the better things got for me, the worse I felt that I couldn't do anything for her, me being helped by her, watching her grow tauter and tauter, watching her die slowly as the strain tightened, and not being able to do anything, not anything, not even understand the struggle as she did. You see, she knew exactly where she stood with life, and she believed things that hurt her. She faced it, and I didn't know the beginning of it. It's only now maybe that I think I see something, but that doesn't matter, she's dead."

He kept talking, he was talking out an elegy; and Henderson listened, looking for the off-key fact, but hearing a man he knew was reaching some sort of stature.

4
THE PAST

The first thing she felt was a sudden and gentle sensation of light; but it wasn't light, because it grew more and more into something else; and then she knew it was consciousness. She awoke from a deep sleep, dimly aware that something must have awakened her, and slowly she came to notice that he was sitting in a straight chair looking at her.

For the moment, she thought she was at Latimer's and almost dismissed the fact of his being there. But the silence held her, silence that meant no one was around. She was going to tell him that Meg must be in the other room, but that didn't seem to fit, and he didn't appear to be concerned.

He was just sitting there, he wasn't smiling, or leering, he wasn't even curious. He had been waiting, it seemed, casually and indifferently, like a man reading a paper on a park bench; he was still waiting: he didn't speak or uncross his legs.

As she sat up, she realized she was in her own apartment: it was like having him next to her soul.

His eyes were wide and heavy lidded, and could have been gentle, but they looked at her from a handsome face that somehow couldn't hide its ruthlessness. The impression remained, despite the blond hair, the chubbiness, the careful clothes, the general tone of a man at a cocktail party.

"How did you get in here?" was the first thing she heard herself say.

"Don't be silly," he replied as if she should have known.

In the silence that followed, she was becoming oriented: she remembered that Jimmy had gone after breakfast; that had been around ten; she looked at her watch: it was four in the afternoon, afternoon because there was daylight behind the venetian; broad daylight, and he was here, without a key, unless Jimmy...; she vaguely recalled a small shiny automatic he had put somewhere, but something told her that nothing could be of any use now. She tried to place the man, but couldn't yet.

"Maybe you've made some sort of mistake," she ventured, getting more alert, "you'd better go."

"No, I'm here to talk to you." He spoke like a man who couldn't be believed.

"You might make a bigger mistake by staying. If I tell the right person about you, you'll be sorry you ever thought of it."

"Who's the right person? Meg Latimer?" He smiled as he said this. "And who does she tell? The people who handle the trouble? That's me, honey. You better wake up."

She placed him now.

"Alright," she said, "wait in the living room. I'll get dressed, it won't take...."

"Go ahead and get dressed," he said and

didn't move.

"Wait in the living room."

He got up and walked out; it wasn't an important point. As soon as he was gone, she went to the door and closed it—a ritual gesture, she knew, void of significance, but it helped her to collect her thoughts.

There was no strategy she could devise, no bargaining points; he was one of the "important people" who had called on Meg, who had only gotten a passing look at her in the garage and who now wanted something of her; the important people who could make Meg nervous and frightened, even Meg, the people who ruled her. She tried to wash and dress with deliberation to dispel the fear that had taken shape, but the idea of the blond man in the living room prevented her. She shouldn't be this afraid, she reasoned, it was all part of her life, as harmless as routine; someone like those two had to exist. She knew Meg took orders from somebody, here's one of them, it's that simple, nothing's changed, nothing: except this place, it's no place now, every place will be no place now, and I've changed, I don't want to go on, and I'm all theirs, all theirs.

She was surprised at her own fear and upset that it should be so great; the feeling of dread possessed her like a theme, a force that gives tone to everything else, a deep disturbance within, irrational, unexaminable, a thing that colored even innocent objects with the power to create fear in her. She felt it as excitement and a near trembling.

She didn't do anything about it, she couldn't; it was too active to allow her to take thought, and not pleasant enough to be accepted as premonition. She examined herself in the dresser mirror; and heartened by the solidity of the image there, she went out into the living room.

"You don't leave much stuff around," he said, "smart."

"What is it you want to tell me?"

"No rush. First, I check."

"I suppose breaking in here is one of the ways."

He smiled his neighborly smile.

"It's a way," he said.

"Well, if you're through checking..." she said, wondering if he had time to see Jimmy's room.

"In the garage," the man said, "he saw you." He made it sound as if someone had been peeping.

She kept silent, waiting for the rest.

"He decided you were it."

"Oh. What does that mean?"

"He just decided. He does things like that, every now and then. That's why I check."

"Alright, what did he decide?"

"He knows, I don't. So stop asking. He said you were it."

"He doesn't even know me."

"He doesn't have to. He saw you. He...Look, honey, don't be stupid, you just be a good girl and do as you're told."

"I haven't been told much so far. Like who you are and who he is."

"So far I'm telling you to be a safe risk: that's my end of it."

"I'm that already. If Meg is satisfied, that should be good enough for you. Is that all you have to tell me?"

"No. What's your dosage?"

"Is this you asking?"

"Him. Answer me."

She told him.

"Increase that, by a third, as fast as you can. I'll be around to check."

"Look, I couldn't get off it anyway, what more do you want?"

"Him, him, it's him that wants, not me. Just do it."

"Is that all?"

"No."

"There isn't much more I can do."

"This is easy. He wants data on you, every-thing, real name, parents, birthplace, friends, any record, everything, understand?"

"Yes."

"Then you wait. Don't be away from here or Latimer's for more than a few hours during the day. You'll be phoned, by Meg, or by one of us. If I call, I'm Herby Lefram; if he calls, he's Mr. Keerson."

"Will this be soon?"

"You never can tell, with him. Just be ready. Take it serious, honey, like a life's work."

With another smile, that looked like a gesture to cover up a helplessness, he walked out and left the door for her to close.

The sun burned down into everything and made the road dance ahead of them. They crossed a bridge, leaving the city, and saw the bathers below intent on comfort from the heat;

they drifted past the holiday noises, the carni-
val-like motels, a few flaccid restaurants dealing
in necessities until someone with more enter-
prise would deal in luxuries, summer lean-to's
doing business in fruits and vegetables and bait,
and some in home-made booze, and some in
phone calls to the big bad city for a little pack-
aged fun, past large and then lone gas stations
with signs a 3rd-grader might have painted,
housing developments on what had been farmland, and on into the receding country.

Going for a drive seemed the only thing to
do; she had to make the time go by and it had to
be done without mere waiting. Impatience
didn't enter into it, nor worry; it wasn't like
waiting for a train or standing around a hospital
for news of an operation; it didn't contain the
bitterness, the petty frustration of being just
idle. She really didn't know what it was like and
she didn't try to formulate it; something irrevo-
cable was about to happen, like a grim mar-
riage; it was being prepared for somewhere;
even she was preparing. She had begun what
felt like confession; she had written, "My name
is...." and stopped to wonder about the identity
of the person who bore her name. And the night

passed till now, Monday, when Jimmy was driving the car along a highway she had mentioned.

She relaxed, at least physically, into the motion of the ride, the changing scenery, the powerful privacy of the big car; and the semi-alertness it all created made her vaguely aware of her thoughts. She wanted to be able to think at her own choosing, not be ridden by fear-created images and the impulses to a flight that was impossible. A decision could be made this way, a decision that attracted her and promised peace, that already made her feel distant and detached from life and from herself, an attractive idea, an idea with power all its own, like a kind of love. It could sustain her through this new turn of events, and then....Panic again: what if this doesn't do it? what if it just looks good now and turns sour like all else when it comes near? She felt the longing and the fear of action that comes with great pain; all the power possible to a human, concentrated into one screamingly desired wish, the wish to be something else, the need, all this she knew to be the measure of her impotence: the great longing and the great impossibility.

At that moment, with the clarity of hallucination, she felt again the terrible, solitary, engulfing pain of the first time she had to walk through the city streets when, after going from "tea to H" —after having broken off to go home and off the stuff and away from him—she returned looking for him with love yet alive but her need greater than all else, walking desperately from place to place where they had had parties and lived and loved and felt like newly created spirits capable of making a new universe, and finding him and crumpling in his arms in joy and welcome and anticipation of relief, and him saying "I've got none, I've got none, we need money" and still not understanding even when she got relief and promised to work for some money, and did so "through friends," and still clung to a hope, thinking that he needed as she needed—and then the dawning, the inevitable facts, the real words describing real things, the discovered baseness behind what to her had been the glory of a free, an unfettered love.

They entered a small town that looked deserted; the inactivity of a hot Monday afternoon when kids take naps or go swimming and people return to work as though going in hid-

ing and parked cars look like ovens in the sun.
She tried to turn her attention outward, but
there wasn't much to hold it, a few not quite
city-looking restaurants, the cluttered store
fronts that reminded her of greed, the usual
two hotels with small tentative neon signs that
announced a drinking room that probably had
kitchen tables in it, the square wooden houses
getting as much rent as they could, the proud
drugstores, the two dusty-looking theatres, the
ivy-covered one-story factory, and the rest that
she knew lay beyond the main street. It all
meant loneliness to her, she had come from a
small town; and she had no real desire to go
back: it was impossible anyway.

"My name is..." was all she had been able to
put down because a whole life was contained in
the words that had to follow; to sound the
name was to call into existence all that she was,
a totality that always would be, the consciousness, the joy, the pain, the evil, the simple being
from day to day, all, all her, concrete, real, existing now, and known by a name, her name, and
known by no one but....The data she had to
write felt like judgment: Mr. Keerson wanted to
know—her. Even Meg didn't know her, Meg

who understood, who, though for her own purposes, took her from the semi-civilized and
part-psychotic fringe underworld where pleas
and tears from beautiful young flesh were part
of the kicks, even Meg, who had shared the
same pain and organized it into a partly live-
able life, couldn't touch the identity summarized by her name. But Mr. Keerson wanted to.
He wanted her exposed and helpless and
owned, the way the cheap sadists had had her:
the top was a lot like the bottom.

Jimmy drove well, and was going fast
enough to avoid tedium, passing the trucks and
letting the speeders pass him. He was making
good time on the uncrowded road, just driving
and not saying anything. She hardly noticed
where they were; and as time passed and the
distance grew, the distraction offered by the
drive wore off and she began to feel unsafe. The
scenery became familiar: a new bridge where
she remembered an old one, a railroad line that
would lead to storage sheds just outside the
town, pretty soon they would come to a soft-
drink factory, and an old decaying mansion just
outside the limits about which they had told
stories as children, and then the sign "Wel-

come": and she knew she'd be home.

She had known it all along; from the moment she had told Jimmy to take that highway, until now when she was admitting it to herself, she had known she would come here; but known it hidingly, like a sort of treachery one would set in motion and shut off the corner of the mind where clarity dwelt: if I could be there, I'd look and make a kind of good-bye and say I'm sorry; but I'd never go, I could never go; still if I were there....They were passing the storage sheds, the factory, the old mansion, the big "Welcome," and the official sign that read "Nordville, 30 mph."

It was a larger small town, with a busy main street and a few proud impersonal touches of the big city; Jimmy eased the car through the bicycle-like traffic without blowing the horn: they were attracting enough attention with the Lincoln alone. When they were through the congested strip, she had him turn off the main street; and when they were near the outskirts, in a residential section that bordered on rolling, well-kept farmland, she asked him to park; and she looked down the street at a wide two-story house with an ivy-covered veranda running along two walls.

It wasn't what she had thought, nor what she had feared; it wasn't the image she had in her memory, it was truer, yes, and the real thing; but there were also too many other things around for it to have the force it had in her imagination. Her memory was from the inside of that house, the way the street looked from the veranda, the countryside from the upstairs window, the trees in the rain—and the outside was a warm image without detail that had simply meant home. As she looked at it, it became like any other house, and she wondered if the hard and very human man who lived there, the man who was her father, would also be eroded by the past years into just another aging man. She knew she could go to him, she knew he didn't share the starchiness of the religion around him, she knew too that this was as far as she'd go; she hadn't seen him since she met Meg six years ago, and she wasn't going to now when the end was in sight: he would never know. It wouldn't do any good if he did, she was out of the reach of human love.

"This is far enough, Jimmy. Let's go back."

He let the car move almost imperceptibly and kept looking through the mirror at the grey car behind them. It had parked about a block away just after they had, and no one had gotten out. He turned at the first cross street to get back to the main street and the highway; and in a few blocks' time the grey car appeared again.

About five miles out, it was the only car behind them.

"That grey car," he said to Elizabeth, "it's probably following us."

She turned and looked.

"Yes, I should have known."

"What shall we do?"

"Nothing now. When we get in town, lose him and take a cab. Make sure nobody sees you going into the apartment. Use the door chain."

"Police?"

"No. Friends, making sure."

"He's been following me all morning."

In a traffic tie-up in the noon congestion, Jimmy had slipped away into a crowd of people boarding buses, and she had led the grey car to Rotsley Avenue.

Meg was acting cautiously; she seemed irritated at being drawn into the situation.

"Of course," she said, "you should have

expected it."

Elizabeth went to the window to look out.

"Get away from there!" Meg snapped at her; and she obeyed. Meg continued in a carefully easy manner, "If he sees you sneaking a look outside, he'll have to think you're trying to get away with something."

As she walked from the window, she realized that Meg was frightened for herself; her hard authority was fear now, a fear that made everyone else a potential threat. Elizabeth had dimly hoped that Meg could supply a little more information, something that might neutralize her own dread, a word of advice maybe—Meg had been around a long time—or even a warning or some idea of the odds; but Meg's attitude only confirmed her hopelessness.

"Maybe he's gone anyway," said Elizabeth to ease the strain.

"I didn't think you'd be coming up here, chicken," said Meg, the old self trying to talk.

"I haven't stopped living here, Meg. We're not strangers, are we?" She was going to say: we're friends; but the phrase seemed so remote now when the full reality of their lives was asserting itself.

"To him, everybody's strangers."

"And to you, Meg? Am I a stranger?"

After a long pause, Meg said, "You have to be."

"Meg, listen: if there's any way out, any way, you've got to tell me."

"There isn't any way out."

"Meg,..."

"What are you so scared about? You don't even know what the deal is. It can't be that bad. You might even get used to it."

Here it was, the phoney talk, encouragement to the sucker. Why had she hoped for anything from Meg? People who weren't involved, the outsiders, couldn't help; they didn't know—but those who did know, the insiders, the ones who were in....All they could do was help you stay in. There had always been a difference, attributed to temperament, between Elizabeth and the others; she knew it now to be a chasm, the depth of a lost humanity, that committed her to bridging it once and for all, alone. The dark was growing, the juggler couldn't see any more.

"It'll work out," Meg was saying. "Hell, after Lefram checks, you can always start cutting down again; it can be done."

"You know about that."

"Sure. He asked me what I was giving you."

"And the other thing? What they're going to phone about, you know that too?"

"Nobody knows about that."

"I guess I'd better be going, Meg," said Elizabeth, and, as though to be sure, asked again, "Is there anything you might want to tell me? We did alright before, you and I."

"Sorry, kid. I'm not in charge of things. They might have been different if Sandra hadn't disappeared."

"Sandra."

"He was interested in her. He likes them young."

She signed the five cheques that remained in her chequebook and placed it, with the two insurances, in the large envelope on the table. Her bankbook recorded a little under nine thousand dollars; there were two amounts in the withdrawal column that could be traced to Dr. Hildebrand, and from her the line to Sandra wouldn't be difficult to establish; even someone who knew only what bank she used could, with help, find these entries. She put the bankbook in the envelope with the other things, and tore off a sheet of note paper which she laid directly on the hard-topped kitchen table. She wrote the date and city and "Dear Dr. Hildebrand: In case you need it, this will authorize you to use the things I am sending you." She signed it carefully and re-read it, deciding again not to mention Sandra; it might never reach Dr. Hildebrand. She looked at everything once more, hesitating, dwelling on possibilities and alternatives, but the course was set: this at least was workable, there would be nothing to find. She sealed the envelope and put it in her handbag.

In the bedroom, she did a hurried examination of her clothes and make-up, anxious now to be started, but the tightly set face she saw in the mirror held her back. Slowly, she forced her features to relax, her eyes to become less narrowed, her lips less compressed; she didn't try to smile: it wasn't happiness she wanted to register, just the neutral indifference of going out, of not being desperate, not being anything. She left the apartment and went out into the street without seeing anyone and without looking around.

She walked the few blocks to a downtown main street and continued strolling until she came to a restaurant where she knew there was a phone in the washroom. She bought a newspaper at the counter, picked the first small table, and sat down with the paper in front of her. It was eight o'clock; the street outside was dimming and looked even darker from the inside of the brightly lit restaurant; there weren't many people eating at this hour and none of them seemed interested in anything but their food; the men looked at her in the usual way; no cars pulled up outside. She ordered a salad and coffee, something already prepared to shorten the time. When it came, she forced herself to eat everything and concentrate on the paper; time passed to eight-fifteen when she got up and went to the washroom.

She dialed Dr. Hildebrand's number. She was in luck.

"Hello."

"Dr. Hildebrand?"

"Yes."

"This is Elizabeth Lucy."

"Yes."

"I haven't much time. I need your help on something."

"What is it?"

"I want to get something to you. Something for...."

"Yes, I understand."

"It's quite a bit, I...If you could..." She felt herself getting confused and losing her nerve; she was thinking of hanging up when Dr. Hildebrand said:

"Elizabeth, I'll take whatever it is and keep it for you."

"I can't go to your place, and I'm afraid to be seen mailing it. Could you have someone meet me?"

"I think so." She could hear muffled talk at the other end. "Yes, I have a friend here from out of town who can go."

"Coming into the city, south, on the new Municipal Road, there's a traffic circle: the first bus-stop before the circle, there's a green shelter there."

Dr. Hildebrand repeated the directions.

"At what time?" she asked.

"In about an hour, say nine-thirty."

There was more muffled talk, a "yes, oh yes," and Dr. Hildebrand said, "You're to look for a '57 Chevrolet with red plates, a blue car."

"Thanks, Doctor."

"Good luck, Elizabeth."

Again the troubled face in the mirror that needed calming: the first part was over. She went back to her table to get the newspaper and the check, trying to look as if she had nowhere to go; she paid at the counter and walked out.

The theatre page said that the program at the Regal Theatre changed at 8:27. A block away, she could see the people streaming out and the short line-up outside; she joined it when she got there, bought a ticket mechanically, and moved with the crowd into the air-conditioned darkness. Once inside, she made her way across the back of the theatre, came out again on the other side of the lobby, and mixed with the people leaving by the side exit.

She slipped into a parked cab and named an intersection not far from where she was going. It would be dark soon, lights were beginning to come on.

The pedestrian-shelter at the bus-stop stood a little way from the traffic circle; the main road had been widened to cover the old suburban street-car tracks and the wooden shelter was allowed to remain standing; they even left the lone light-bulb on the telephone pole next to it while not far away the traffic circle blazed with bluish modern lighting; next to the shelter was a hasty park of shrubbery and benches replacing

the hay patches that had grown along the street-
car line; the region was largely industrial, the
clean industries, jammed with people in the rush
hours and steady with permanent traffic at night.

She was sitting on a park bench, facing the
road and watching the cars. It was dark now,
summer dark, close to nine-thirty when the
lights look energetic against a still visible sky.
Headlights streamed along the road and
swirled in the circle, the drivers hidden and the
whole scene strangely unpeopled; a slow
freight puffed along an overpass where the cars
disappeared; all around, the huge industrial
signs and floodlit spaces created a glow in the
deepening night; and when the noise subsided,
as it did in spasms, the light too seemed to
become quiet.

She was sure no one had followed her, but
she had no way of finding out. Looking around
would make her conspicuous and over aware
of everything except real danger; she only
wanted to do this one thing safely; it was
almost impersonal: Lefram's vague terrorizing
could only go so far, he needed her unmarked,
and unscarred, and above all, alive. If she were
a threat to the rackets, he would probably have

to kill her; but at any moment now, that trail would be covered over. And she'd be free to encounter the world that created Lefram: the world she had just missed earlier: the specialty houses, the private movie-making, the breaking in of newly hooked kids whose value was high for a brief time only: a world where the turnover was as fast as the arrests, the breakdowns, the suicides.

A big construction truck, full of rock, sputtered and hissed to make a turn where she was waiting. The noise distracted her and the ground shook with the effort. When she turned to resume her watching she was looking at a blue car that was idling in line with the shelter. As she got up, she noticed the red plates with white lettering.

She got in, and the car moved on.

"I'm Sister Hildebrand's friend," he said. "You're Elizabeth Lucy?"

"Yes."

He was about forty: his hair made him look young—black, wavy, and combed back; but his face was lined and furrowed, calm in a way that betrayed a past strain, with steady knowing eyes that could easily have been hard. He was wearing a white sports shirt; and when he reached toward the ash tray in the dash, she saw that his hands were lean and well-kept.

She didn't say anything more; she felt base at her own caution, but anyone who knew the surface facts could say "Sister" and not "Doctor."

As if he felt her worry, he said, "I'm on vacation up here; I visit the doctor's place whenever I get a chance. I've been able to talk to Sandra a few times. She's doing alright."

He turned into a drive-in restaurant and said, "Cokes," to the waitress just for the sake of ordering something.

"It's better than parking on a street," he said, "here we're tourists."

"Are you a doctor?"

"No."

She gave him the envelope which he stuffed into a brief-case he had in the back seat.

"There's a railroad station nearby," she explained, "I'll get off there and take a cab."

"You in a hurry?"

"No, just anxious to get it finished."

"Sister thought you might want to talk about things."

"That's very kind," she said, almost defeated by the naïveté, and in a way glad that it existed. "But why should I talk to you?"

"I'm a priest."

It was like hearing a last bolt slam shut: the unchangeable past, the unchangeable future. A handcuff snapping on her wrist couldn't have been more definite.

She said without irony, "Dr. Hildebrand likes to come to the point, doesn't she?"

"She's like that, yes. But this is an accident. I'd just come back from a golf game when you called. She's not prying, nor am I. I'm here, that's all."

"She tell you anything?"

"Some. But I've been talking with Sandra."

"It's worse with me, all around. You can't begin to understand how it is."

"I can understand some of it," he said.

"No," she whispered, "you can't. Not from the inside. The helplessness. The pain."

He lit another cigarette. And looking straight ahead, he exhaled smoke and said, "For what it's worth: I'm an alcoholic. I'm off the liquor, but I'll always be one."

He didn't press the point, he just sat there. She was grateful for the confidence, his act of abasement to show her she wasn't alone. But it couldn't change anything. They sat in silence, looking inside the restaurant at the energetic gaiety of early evening, the not yet tired staff smiling properly, the general air of holiday: summer happiness.

"You've heard the others," he began saying in a quiet voice, "you've heard them justifying themselves, saying this or that was natural and good and unavoidable, or that everybody had a racket anyway, or why be a hypocrite, eh? You've heard all this, kidding themselves, even the 'good' people, about a phoney innocence."

"Yes."

"You're not doing it."

"Why should I? I can see."

"That's right. You can look right at it. Some people don't even get that far. Don't you think that kind of clarity could be a grace?"

"It doesn't change things."

"It already has, in a way."

"Are you trying to tell me to go off the habit?"

"I'm trying to tell you the habit doesn't make that much difference."

"What will make the difference?"

"You, for one thing. The rest I don't know. It's your life: you'll know at one point."

"I'm not there yet."

He started the car and drove her to the railroad station she had mentioned.

"I could hear your confession," he said.

"No," she replied, "I can't even do that. Thanks for helping. Good-bye...Father."

"Good-bye, Elizabeth."

She got out and walked toward the waiting cabs. He pulled away and raised his hand in benediction after her as though blessing the night.

She was on a road beckoning to a lone figure in the distance and saying: closer, come closer, I can't hear what you're saying. You've got to come closer. The figure had no face, just a voice that she felt as the pressure of intention, not a verbal message; and it had no real form, only an outline that kept changing whenever she addressed it: it receded or shrank when she spoke in that direction, and approached when she was silent, each move taking a long time and being done slowly and heavily like boring music, resisting all her efforts to hurry things, gliding passively and laboriously, unaware of any urgency. As this continued, she grew certain that the figure wasn't moving at all: she was the one, working with so much effort and going contrary to the consequences she intended.

There was a house, inside, an apartment, Meg's. She was alone in it; Meg wasn't around, and someone was coming; it was late. This has happened before, she wanted to say, I know this has happened before. She tried to leave and couldn't. But this has happened before, I don't have to stay. On the street, which she could see easily as though there were no walls, a girl ran wet with tears—and she knew she was waiting for Sandra. Again. It can't be happening again; she didn't leave....And she was holding her in her arms and trying to stop the young girl from sobbing her way into death. Liz, he wanted me to....And I couldn't, I ran out, we fought, I've got to get away, get away, get....This did happen before. How...? Sandra, Sandra, where is he, where is he, where is he...? Here's your money, buster, you make trouble and you'll wind up dead. Lights in the rain, flight, don't take a fix now, let it ride, kid, let it ride, take it straight from now on, take the shock this way, if you feel less like dying later you might want to live, we'll find a way, how much've you been taking? Sandra, Sandra, you, innocence and fresh beauty, Sandra, where...?

A male presence said: it's all forgiven, you can go now. Go where? Just go, come on, move, you can't stay here, you're on the way up, honey, go, forget about Sandra. How do you know about her? She was running toward the figure on the road, trying to spin and turn around in mid-air so that she could carry out her intention of running away.

It was a nice day at the end of the road, she was feeling gay and free, though she didn't know what she was, beyond being something that could feel. But it was a nice day. They were turning on the sun for her, and bringing her the summer-morning air, alive with the smell of flowers and the sounds of birds. They were nice people, all smiling and happy, and concerned about her; the sunlight reached the dark corners, and the doors were open to the air; and as this happiness permeated the building, she was looking for herself: she knew she was there, she was herself, but where was that self? You can go. It was another voice now. Go? Yes, go; we've opened the sun and the air, and the doors, and we've taken down the bars, can't you see? The building began to take shape, from the inside growing out; and it became concrete and metal, a prison, clean and gleaming, full of light and air. Yes, I see. But where am *I*? She tried to move and got no response from what she remembered as her body. She tried and tried, and the building didn't move. Why should the building move? And she tried again to move the building, and she realized that she was really trying to move her body. She was the building, the prison....To hell with you, nice people.

Running now, tired, about to fall down any minute. It was getting hot, feverish, and the road was gone, and stones got in the way. She looked up from her efforts and saw a vast wasteland that seemed to heave with the heat of the setting sun. She saw a man there who was hungry, but she paid no attention to him. Her work was too much: she was carrying a stone now, the building had become the stone; she couldn't hold it any more. She let it fall and stayed there with it, resting; and when she got up again, she couldn't lift it, and the sun was gone, and all she knew was the night and the unliftable stone in the wasteland. She called out to the man she had seen, but only heavy distorted echoes came back; she kept calling, not naming a name but calling a person all the same, a searching desperate utterance in the dark fastened to a stone that she knew by touch. The echoes travelled on and on, getting heavier, and changing into other sounds, the groan of time passing, the fall of the years behind the sun. She couldn't hear herself calling any more as the dark rocky wasteland grew into the sounds of frightful combat and the agonizing screams of perpetual defeat.

A bell is ringing now over the countryside, a new and different land, but it's ringing without reason. It's getting faster, the strokes are rapid, not rung by hand, too fast for strokes, becoming steady like....

The phone woke her. She sat up and took some time to believe she was in her apartment; it was morning, nine-fifteen by the clock on the dresser. The phone kept calling her. She concentrated on its ringing, still conscious of a stone in a wasteland, a fading image that left her when she began walking to the phone.

"It's me," said Meg's voice. "You're to get here by 10:30 tonight."

5

THE PRESENT

It was late afternoon before Henderson could leave the city. He was driving with his coat off and his sports shirt out to cover his holster. The traffic was beginning to build up; people were let out of work early in the heat, and they made their way to the beaches and the golf courses on the edge of the city. At the bridge, there were delays as a policeman directed traffic alternately to it and to the beach road. The tie-up continued to the other side, and finally vanished as Henderson drove by the housing development and into the country. A call had come in the night before from a town called Nordville: a man inquiring about the death of Elizabeth Lucy; he hadn't left his name. The call had been traced to a phone booth on the town's main street.

The drive took an hour and a half. Past the welcome sign, Henderson stopped for gas and put his coat back on. He got into a phone booth and looked at the book. There was no Marc Lapier, photos. His idea was fading fast, maybe he was in the wrong town. The only photography store listed was a "Harry's Camera Supplies" on the main street.

Deciding to postpone supper, he drove slowly up the main street and looked on both sides at the stores. Cars honked at him to move and roared by impatiently when he didn't, only to be stopped by one of the many traffic lights: they needed them in this town. At the third light, he saw the camera supply shop; it was a branch of a large firm and took up the corner of what looked like a busy intersection. He parked, crossed the street, and went in.

A girl came out of the back and said, "Yes, sir?"

"Do you know if there's a photographer in town called Marc Lapier?"

"Well, no. But there used to be. He died a few years ago, something he got in the war. You can't know him very well."

"I don't know him at all. Thanks."

Another look at a phone book told him where to find the newspaper office. He drove back up the main street and turned off into a side street where he saw a three-story building with stone arches for window frames and a large sign announcing the "Nordville Chronicle."

Behind a low glass partition with "editor" painted on it, a man in his thirties sat looking through a small stack of newspapers. His white shirt was open at the neck, and a bow tie hung from one of the collar tips.

"Are you the editor?" asked Henderson.

"Managing editor," the man said, "my name's Pile, no relation, different spelling. What do I think I can do for you?"

"I'm trying to locate somebody who might be in this town. All I've got's a picture."

"You're a cop. Let's see it."

Henderson gave him the picture of the aging man on the porch steps. Pile looked at it and turned it over.

"Well?" urged Henderson.

"What do you want him for?"

"Not a damn thing. I can't even make out a traffic ticket out here. He might be able to identify somebody."

"That's Colonel Denis, retired, distinguished war record, owns property here, interested in civil defense. Used to be interested in politics, but he gave it up."

"Where will I find him?"

Pile handed him a battered phone book. "G. Denis on St. Michael Street." Henderson found it and thanked him. As he was leaving, Pile's voice followed him, "Whatever it is, go easy on him. He's tough, but not that tough."

"Yeah."

He drove out to the number. There was nobody home. He decided it was time for supper.

In a little under two hours, Henderson had tried the house three times, only to find it still empty. But the car he had seen in the driveway kept him coming. By the fourth time, it was dark; he had to approach with his headlights on. He got out of the car and started up the walk. There were no lights on in the house; about half a block away, a street light shone enough for him to see the place. A small breeze rustled the vines covering the long veranda, and his footfall on the steps seemed louder than it should have been. When he was on the second stair, a man said: "That's as far as you're going. Another step and I'll fire."

He froze, and waited. When he was looking in the right direction into the shadows on the veranda, he saw the sten-gun. A grey-haired man was behind it, sitting in an upright lawn chair, not moving.

"I've been expecting somebody to show up, somebody from her circle." The voice was hard with restraint, but calm. "You took too long. Yesterday I would have shot you getting out of the car. Today, I'll hear you out."

Henderson started to say something and moved as he did so.

"No," the man said. "Open your coat wide and keep holding it."

He came down and took Henderson's gun.

"Good thing you didn't shoot, Mr. Denis,"

said Henderson. "I'm with homicide, in Montreal, my name's Henderson."

The man took Henderson's wallet. When he was close, Henderson could see that his eyes were wet. On seeing the badge, the man returned the wallet and the gun. Henderson adjusted his coat.

"I...I must apologize, Mr. Henderson. I expected the police earlier, they didn't come. I see you already know my name."

"I didn't think I knew who she was till now. That sten won't do you any good, or her."

"It could give me some satisfaction. And wouldn't it be right, to destroy those who destroyed her? Never mind, it's a purely rhetorical question. A matter of feeling with me. Won't you come in?"

He led the way into the house and into the kitchen, turning on lights as he went. He uncocked the sten and removed the magazine; he put both pieces on the sink.

"We may as well sit in here, it's cooler. Will you have a glass of beer with me, Mr. Henderson?"

"Yes, of course."

As he poured it, he said, "You're here to ask me questions; I understand your position. So please do, in the right language. You needn't choose soft words on my account."

"When did you find out she was dead?"

"Last night. About eight-thirty. A man phoned, he said my daughter had died the night before, and that he thought I'd want to be informed."

"Did he use those words?"

"No, he said, 'I sorta thought you'd like to know.'"

"Where did the call come from, do you know?"

"I have no idea. But it was long distance: I heard a few coins ringing. I went out then, and got the city papers. They had an item about her, they called her Elizabeth Lucy, those were her first names. They said she probably committed suicide. I wasn't ready to believe that, not after that phone call. And on the assumption that if one could call, another might turn up thinking she had told me things, or left something with me, I called up the city morgue, so that they'd keep her for me. But I didn't call you people. My feelings ran away with me, I thought I could confront them, whoever they are, alone with a swifter justice. But who could I confront, if she did commit suicide?"

"She may have. I don't know yet."

"What's your opinion?"

"I don't think she did," Henderson allowed the man that little comfort, "although what I've found out doesn't exclude it."

"Then she may have been murdered." He wasn't pressing for confirmation of any preconception, he only wanted to know.

"I don't know," replied Henderson. "It may have been an accident. There may have been a fight of some sort. That kind of party can change to anything."

"Party? What do you mean by that?"

"How much do you know about her, Mr. Denis?"

"Nothing really. But I can surmise. I have surmised. I've never investigated. She only came here once since...since she left for good. She visited me about five years ago, I'm not sure. She said to me, 'I just wanted to see you, dad, as one person to another, without discussing me' and we chatted a short while. She took along my picture on leaving. Her silence told me of her life, nothing exact, but all I had to know. I knew that if she could make it different, she would; if she didn't, it was because she was in too far. It's easy to get involved, Mr. Henderson, I bear her no grudges: how could I grudge her her own pain? Maybe now, you should tell me the details she and I passed over...."

Henderson drank some of his beer as he looked for the words he knew he couldn't find.

"She was a prostitute," he said, "part of a girl service, but not small time. What kept her there was that she was an addict. When she died, she was wearing an evening dress. That's why I said 'party' a moment ago. No real witness has turned up. We're still looking."

"Not a very nice affair."

Henderson sipped from his glass. He didn't say anything more.

"I kept seeing her today as a little girl; I was down by the school tonight. Small, very eager, innocent. Very open, human. She retained that, you know; she could always face things. She was lovely as a girl, and beautiful as a woman. Through the war I remembered her all the time, a warm existence that was home. It's...it's overwhelming that such a person should cease to be—and in that fashion—it's too much. Well, she's dead. That much is certain. I've prayed for her all along. That too is certain. Maybe her sins won't rest too heavily on her head...."

151

Henderson let the man speak it out. He stayed longer than he had expected, listening, feeling the dimension of the man's grief. He didn't tell him about Jimmy, nor that she had been here a few days before and looked at his house. He had been told enough about his daughter. About an hour later he left and registered at a hotel.

The Bestview Motel looked out over a wide lake and was probably as cool as the sign promised when the sun went down. Most of the log-cabined units had cars in front of them, and from behind Henderson could hear the noises of people at the beach. He was eighty miles from Nordville and at the place closest to the highway phone booth where someone had called her father the night before. The local police had little trouble tracing it; and the chief, who knew Colonel Denis, hadn't insisted on being told the history of the case.

The day wasn't as hot as usual yet, and clouds were forming in the distance over the hills across the lake. A few women in shorts strung quick washings on the umbrella-like stands the motel seemed to provide; a milkman, who had everything including live chickens in his truck, was making his way around to the beach: the just-like-home touch, have a barbecue, we kill them, you have the fun. In the wooded area there were tents with the motel's name on them; it was a good idea; it looked like a rare treat, and it was cheaper than building additional units.

The proprietor looked like an energetic man who was turning fat. He was wearing nothing but shorts and he seemed to know business was going well.

"I get lots of people," he was saying to Henderson's questions. "For one night, one hour, anything. It's kinda hard to remember everybody."

"This would have been yesterday, or the night before that."

"Can you describe him?"

"No. He may have been a light-haired man, chubby."

"I don't think there was anybody here like that. Three families came in yesterday. An old couple night before that. Lots of people to eat and to use the beach."

"Any other places around here?"

The man beamed. "Not for eight miles. This place is competition, believe me."

"Sure looks like it. Thanks."

"Any time, any time."

Henderson got back into the heat of the car and drove the eight miles. The aging couple who ran a few fishing cabins hadn't seen anyone for days and were glad of it. Henderson continued his search to gas stations, a small town's two hotels, anything that looked like a boarding house, garages; he looked at roadside picnic clearings and places where he saw any refuse. He drove on for as long as he thought was compatible with being within easy driving distance of the highway phone near the Bestview Motel.

His map said that a road led from where he was to a lower highway that could lead him back to the city and still cover his theoretical radius. But he felt he had played out his long shot: the man who phoned had probably kept going.

He reached the lower highway, a twisting road through fertile farmland. It was country-quiet now and almost one o'clock. He enjoyed looking at the rough lawns and the big trees in front of the farmhouses; the odd sign invited him to buy fresh eggs; he passed a boy, who smiled, sitting by a vegetable stand in the shade; and in a while the siding changed to a high fence containing well-tilled land; in the distance he saw buildings: huge barns and a white stone church that looked like a cathedral. He recognized the monastery and decided to turn in to buy some of their cheese for lunch. A few men, in civvies, sat in a park-like grotto; behind the fence on the farm, a monk in a straw hat and clumpy boots caught his eye and smiled with a great nod of his head. Henderson coasted down the driveway and parked.

He changed his mind about the cheese. Under a wooden roofing that probably was once used to accommodate wagons and sleighs was a blue '52 Oldsmobile.

"I can't stay long," Henderson told the guest-master, "perhaps just long enough to make mass in the morning."

The monk smiled and said, "Of course, suit yourself. I'll just have time to show you to your room; we're going to lunch in a few minutes."

"You have lunch late," said Henderson just to chat.

"We're on standard time out here."

Henderson laughed conversationally and added to it: "A friend of mine said he might be up here, a young light-haired man..."

"That would be Mr. Lester perhaps. He arrived yesterday."

"Oh, that's great. Could you give me a room next to his?"

"Right this way. I'll take your...."

"My stuff's in the car. I'll get it later." He followed the monk to the third floor of the guesthouse. Standard time: that means the phone call was made after supper at 7:30; it fitted...if "Mr. Lester" had done the phoning.

"That's Mr. Lester's room, No. 27. Yours is 29. You'll find a time-table on the door to the chapel."

"Thank you, Father."

Henderson went into his room and let the monk go back downstairs. He listened for sounds in the next room, but the wall was too thick. A bell began ringing presumably for lunch. Ignoring room No. 27 entirely, he went downstairs and followed a group of men into the dining hall. A brother smilingly indicated a place for him to sit. They said grace silently.

As the platters of food were passed, Henderson looked around the long table casually. Diagonally opposite him, to his left, sat a blond man with a chubby face that needed a shave. His eyes passed over Henderson long enough to take him in. The meal proceeded in silence. Henderson concentrated on his food and neglected some of the finer points of etiquette; he used his thumb and mopped his plate with bread and wiped his mouth delicately with his fingers and did his best to look like a man only a monastery would tolerate. He passed over the dessert, stood up, and paused the time it took to say grace. When the brother passed him, he hooked him and asked, "Brother, could you tell me where the chapel is?" He was told gladly.

He went back upstairs and into Lefram's room.

A nylon shirt was drying on the back of a rocking chair; several new pairs of socks were on the dresser top along with underwear still in the cellophane wrapping. On the shelf over the sink was a cheap new razor and a hardly squeezed tube of lather. A small canvas travelling bag was on the floor near the bed. There was no clothes closet. Charley Maet hadn't delivered yet.

Men walked in the hall, voices, the toilet went, doors opened and closed. Henderson waited. He didn't wait long. The door opened a little and then all the way, and Lefram walked in. He went wide-eyed at Henderson's gun.

Henderson closed the door with his foot and spun him around.

"Touch the top of the door jamb."

Lefram wasn't armed. Henderson went to the canvas bag and found a gun there. He put it in his coat pocket, searched the bed quickly and said, "Sit on the bed, Herby."

Lefram took his time getting his composure back. He looked at Henderson from head to foot carefully, at the gun that was going back into the holster but remained exposed, at the grey eyes that looked at him with impersonal contempt.

"How do you know who I am?" he asked nervously.

"I bumped into Charley Maet at Keerson's place."

It got a reaction: Lefram stiffened as though he were getting ready to spring. "You're...."

"Don't try it, Herby. Not till you find out."

"Yeah," he muttered with a sigh. "Yeah. Alright, just who are you?"

"The name's Henderson. I'm with homicide. You can tell me things I've been waiting to hear."

"I don't oblige that easily, Henderson."

"You don't have to. I can tie you in with her death without your help."

"Stop crapping me. That's impossible."

"She was seen, leaving the Rotsley Avenue apartment with the Latimer woman in her own car; you were seen, after bringing the car back, with Latimer, after her death. Call it what you want, but that ties you in."

"You're way out. You get Meg Latimer to talk, it'll be a different story."

"I can't. She's dead, two days dead. That leaves you."

"Holy...!"

"You could have killed both of them."

"No! Come on, don't be so damn thickheaded. Would I still be here?"

"Doesn't mean a thing, Herby. Guys like you do funny things. Like phoning her father last night. Not smart, for a guy on the run. And I know people who'll explain that as a guilt reaction. That'll be a real party, won't it, Herby? And cold, with no H to make it look like a dream."

Lefram put his head in his hands and rubbed his face. Henderson moved a chair up against the door and sat there; he slipped the gun out when Lefram said "smokes" and reached in his coat for cigarettes, lit one, and threw the paper match on the floor.

"I had called Charley first," Lefram explained. "He was supposed to get here last night. I was all set to move out, for good. I just thought her father should know about her, that's all."

"That bothered you, eh?"

"OK, OK, what do you know about it? I'm the one who knew her, I knew everything about her. So I just called him. I'm human."

"Yeah."

Lefram looked at the burning cigarette for a while and twirled it around his fingers.

"So you still think I'm it?" he said.

"I haven't heard anything yet."

"That night, he was having one of his 'parties' and..."

"Who?"

"Keerson. He had a real bad yen for her. He'd seen her once. He's a little crazy, that guy. You don't know the effect she had on him. He knew she was, something, not just sex, something...more. I...I can't explain it, it..."

"Just stay with the story."

"Yeah. They came up late that night, the Lucy girl and Latimer. I let them in. I wasn't in on the doings, I was in charge of things on the outside. The doings were in the living room. She was told to go in the bedroom and wait. The only thing I know is that later I saw him go in there, and Latimer followed. Then all the yelling he was doing and us getting out of there."

"Who was in the living room?"

"I don't know."

"You let them in, you ought to know!"

"He kept the place dark. He had candles in the living room."

"What were they doing in there?"

"I don't know, I don't know. That bastard used to even tease me about it."

"All right. You drove Latimer home in the girl's car."

"Yeah. She had her clothes. Then I called Charley from down the street. I didn't have any money on me, just ten bucks! I got some off Meg. I came here, you can get away without paying, and nobody talks to you. That's it, Henderson. Twist it any way you want, but that's it."

"I might buy it. Now, why are you running?"

"I'm through with him. He's crazy. If I get clear of this, I'll....He's crazy. I want to go some place and try to...try to...I can't undo

anything, I know, but...Him and his cute trimmings, kids, young kids, boys, to hell with
him, that's all."

"One thing more: how do I get to him? He's
never around that penthouse."

"No, no, he isn't, not him. He's on the floor
below, in 1125."

"You got a key?"

"No. You don't need one. He'll know you're
coming."

Henderson motioned to Lefram to pack his
things: and when that was done, they left the
room, stopped at the guest-master's empty
office while Henderson put some money on the
desk, and continued on their way to Henderson's car.

"You drive," said Henderson. "Keep it under
fifty."

Lefram got in from the passenger's side. And
as Henderson settled in beside him, a man got
up from a bench in the grotto and half trotted
over with a bouncy step. He sounded pleasant
as he said, "You fellows going into town?"

"Yes," said Henderson, "but that way." He
indicated the opposite direction.

"Fine," said the man, and got into the back seat.

Henderson began to turn around to talk him out of it, but he felt a gun muzzle at his neck and a hand darting his gun from his holster.

"Who's this gizmo, Herby?"

"Cop."

"Just in time, eh? Good thing Charley got in touch with the right people. What do we do with him?"

"He's got my gun. He...."

Henderson didn't catch the rest; a sharp blow filled his head with pain and he swirled into unconsciousness.

The car was too hot. He didn't know how long it had been in the sun, but it was choking him. He was wet. He could see the sweat stains on the arms of his coat as he tried to push himself upright. The steering wheel got in the way and he fell back to the seat face down.

"There's a gun in the back seat."

"Let's call the police."

"Yes, of course, but let's help him first."

He recognized the voice of the guest-master. A towel with cold chunks in it was put on his neck. He was helped to sit up. The monk got in and started the car. He moved it through the fence gate and into the shade, opened all the doors, and came around to help Henderson out.

"You can stretch out on the grass here, it's cooler."

"You don't have to call the police for me," said Henderson and fished out his wallet. "But you can about a '52 Oldsmobile, with two men, one blond and the other dark-haired and balding, both in their thirties. Also about another car, there must have been another car."

The monk left and returned immediately with Henderson's gun; then he went off to phone. Henderson looked at the tree branches that seemed to be in motion against the moving clouds. He put some of the ice on his face and sat up to wash away the blood on the back of his head. In a few minutes, he got to his feet tentatively and paced around the tree. Who's this gizmo? Charley got in touch. Cop. You don't kill a cop, you just hit him on the head. Lefram seemed to have devoted friends; very comforting in this cold world, touching. Charley was a little slow, though, wasn't he? Good old Charley, he came through, he got in touch with the right people. Or did he? Round and round the tree, and up the garden path. I wish those guys'd stop looking at me.

When the monk came back, Henderson thanked him for everything, and got into the cooled-off car. He backed to the driveway, turned, still being watched by the amazed group, and got onto the highway. It was half past two; he had been unconscious for almost an hour.

A few miles out, as he was getting more confident about his driving, he saw two provincial police cars parked on the shoulder of the road. When he approached he was able to see the officers down the embankment examining a blue car. The doors were open, but they weren't touching anything, and they didn't look as if they were getting ready to tow it. They stood about quietly. One of them was taking notes. He went down and identified himself.

"Guy in it," one of the officers said. "He got it in the face. The shells are in the car. It was probably done with a fully automatic pistol."

Henderson looked at the few clear areas of blond hair and at the flies that buzzed around the spilled life of Herby Lefram.

6
THE PAST

The bartender looked her way with casual noticing eyes, and he seemed disappointed when she didn't accept the smiling offer of the man standing by her table. The man moved himself across the room to take in the singer, and left her watching her coffee like a girl who wasn't having a good time. She could hear the song piercing the air, and feel the pressure of the loud talk under the low ceiling, and see—if she wanted to—the people who were making it; but none of it could really touch her. She hadn't even wanted the coffee; it was just something to have on the table; and the cigarette was just something to have with the coffee. It didn't matter: time had to pass; and waiting was the least worrisome way of making sure it did. She didn't know any more when she'd begin the craving; she couldn't count on her former timing, it had been upset by the additional takes; and she had only one left in her purse.

The old Negro came around, emptying ashtrays and wiping tables.

"That coffee is more'n likely cold. You want me to change it for you?"

She half smiled at him. "No thanks," she said. "I wouldn't drink it anyway."

He nodded, and with a glance around the room, he decided to leave. The singer was going into another song; some people left for other places; some came in; time passed. The bartender watched the attention she was getting: men looked at the light red-tinged hair and around the pale green dress. Her sitting alone made things look possible; nothing much would happen; possibility alone was a satisfying atmosphere.

She watched the little second hand on her watch; it was only a shiny thing going around meaninglessly. She was past the point where caring can do any good. Her fear had lost its edge and become dull like a sort of peace: it stayed on as an unfeeling preoccupation, empty of real content, and ready for a greater void. It made things a lot easier. She didn't have to decide anything; she had no thoughts to collect; and the chaotic images and fantasies that lived at night had no real existence in the thumping nightclub. She had covered herself; she followed instructions; Lefram had his information; it had begun: pick the right card, baby, it's a new beginning with the old deck; you can't lose, they need the players.

The cigarette had burned down to cold ash and the coffee was scummed. She picked up her handbag and put some money on the table. She walked past the crowding chairs with unintended sexiness and made her way out as eyes followed the green movement.

It was 10:30.

She parked on the street in front of the apartment building and went upstairs to number 10.

Meg was sitting on the couch, looking ready to go out, with her purse and a small suit-box on the coffee table in front of her. When she saw Elizabeth, she looked at her watch and nodded a greeting.

Elizabeth kept standing and asked, "Well, Meg, when do I go?"

"I'll be going with you, sit down."

"When will that be?"

"When he phones. We're to wait. Sit down, you look nervous that way."

She sat in an armchair not quite facing Meg, and turned on the radio; it would fill the silence. Meg reached for a magazine and began leafing through it with careful ease; she could have been in a railroad station waiting for a dull relative. The tension mounted all the same; the calm was too elaborate.

"Where will we be going, Meg?"

"Keerson's place. We go in your car."

"How do I get there?"

"I'll direct you."

"This is really careful, eh? I won't know where he lives until I'm involved, is that it?"

"Yeah."

"I suppose the same thing goes for what we're going to do?"

"That's right."

"Don't you think I should know now?"

"He doesn't want it that way."

"Look, I'm here. I've come this far."

"It's not far enough."

"All right, what is far enough?"

"When you can't turn back. That's what far enough is."

Meg was going to say something more, but she stopped talking and looked at the window, staring at her own thoughts. The magazine lost its shape under her hand. Elizabeth watched her controlling whatever it was she had to control.

"Don't make trouble," Meg almost hissed. "You really shouldn't be going. Not *you*." The word was bitten out in what looked like hate. "He wouldn't listen." Silence for a while, and then: "Yeah! He's right. Right. Just who are you for me to think that...? Just another dame. You're like us, all right, what's the difference? A little time. He knows. He knows."

There was nothing to be said after that. Elizabeth got up and went to the room she used—she couldn't think of it as her room—and sat down on the bed trying not to notice the waiting. She heard the paced tones of a newscast; then music, to which she gave all her attention; the presence of rain on the window; the stillness of Meg; and finally the phone ringing over the sound of the radio. Together they left the apartment and went downstairs to the car.

Enough rain was falling to make her use the wipers and concentrate on the reflecting streets. The night had remained hot, and the air was now sticky. The car felt tight, smaller than usual; she put down her window and let the rain come in, and the new air. The rhythm of the wipers was like time running ahead, and she held the car back while Meg's toneless voice issued directions and kept it on its way.

"Go up Hillton Road....On Ellesbry, left....That road behind the building....Cut the lights."

She turned them off and let the car creep ahead. They were passing a line of garage doors. At the second from the end, Meg said, "Here. Keep the motor on."

In a few minutes, the garage door was opened by a man whose face she couldn't see; he shone a flashlight where he wanted her to bring the car and closed the door.

"Leave the keys in. I'll put it away."

She knew him now; it was Herby Lefram. They got out of the car in the dark; he led the way to the elevator, shining the light on the floor. He set the controls, turned off the flashlight, and they rode up in the dark, without a word, passing the lighted halls at each floor, and making it impossible to be seen by anyone who might be waiting outside. At the top, they were again in darkness. They crossed the hall and entered the penthouse. The only thing she could notice was the cool air.

"Wait," said Lefram, and walked away.

A light was coming from somewhere. She edged quietly away from Meg and tried to see; as she moved, the glow brightened and flickered until a candle flame came into view, then another. She couldn't see the rest of the room, and didn't have time to move closer. The beam from a flashlight hit the floor and she moved back.

"In there."

It was a new voice, not loud, somewhat ringy, and sounding as if the speaker was always wetting his lips; it belonged to the man who had returned with Lefram. The light rested on a door which was opened, and Meg walked through with Elizabeth. When the door was finally closed, Meg threw the light switch and began undoing the suit-box she had brought.

The room gave the impression of being larger than it was. It was long, with glass doors at one end leading outdoors, and the few furnishings it had made it look spacious: a huge mirror on the wall behind the bed, a very long dresser, one armchair, a cedar chest near the door, and all toned down by the indirect lighting that ran along the four walls. It didn't look used or lived in; it could have been a sales display.

"You'll put this on," said Meg. "Only this."

She held out folds of sheer white material that looked like a free-fitting evening dress. "This way," she said, and illustrated with a few quick gestures. Elizabeth had to force herself to listen and watch; the only thing she could think of was a store, as if nothing else existed: the idea almost unnerved her: the clear impression of buying things in a store, of going home soon to try them on. She sat on the bed quickly and rubbed her eyes as if to remove the impression.

"Meg...," she began. But Meg was gone.

Slowly, she put her things on the bed near the suit-box and fitted the sheer material around her. She could feel her face getting taut and her eyes aching with repressed tears; she held her hands out and saw that they were still steady enough, but her whole body was on the verge of trembling. The room was becoming uncomfortable. She went to the glass doors, avoiding the mirror as she passed, and opened them. The air was warmer, but she hardly noticed that; she was outside, where it had stopped raining, and where the sky was beginning to show a few stars. The view relaxed the supercharged tone of the room. She looked out without bothering to take note of the time; and not wanting to have her private action discovered, she went back inside.

The room was confining; its cold tones were beginning to upset her. She lay down on the bed and closed her eyes to shut it out, but she knew where she was. Maybe outside again....

The door clicked open.

She sprang up. He stood there, as he eased the door closed, and looked at her with eyes that didn't quite seem to contact hers. His face was strained, young-looking in a pouchy way, and sharp featured. The strain seemed to widen his eyes and stiffen his mouth slightly. The skin on his forehead looked white next to the black hair, but his cheeks and nose had tiny clusters of red marks. Except for his eyes, he could have been any other tired man, not quite old, who felt the effort of living. But he wasn't; she surmised she was dealing with Mr. Keerson.

"In ten minutes, or not much longer," he said in the voice she had heard in the hall, "you are to come in. Someone will tap on the door and you will follow, carrying this."

He handed her a large gold locket and left the room.

It felt sturdy; it was more like an ornamental container of some kind than a locket. It had a gold chain fastened to it and an obvious catch. She opened the catch and pushed back the lid. There was something white in the circular depression. She thought it was heroin at first, but it didn't move when she tilted the locket; it was solid. She heard herself gasp as she realized what it was; she started to tremble and had to hold it with two hands then. She stared at it, incredulous: she was looking at a host.

She slumped to her knees. The room had left her consciousness now. She was aware of very little except the pounding of her heart and the white disc that held her eyes. She began to cry softly, unaware of the tears running down her face. Her voice barely said: I...didn't think...You....She stumbled to her purse, hooked it with her arm, and started to the door.

Someone tapped on it gently.

She fumbled at the locket and couldn't get her fingers to work. She turned it over and let the host fall into the palm of her hand. And then she pressed it into her mouth as if she were drinking water from a stream. She was aware of a wasteland somewhere, and a name, and....

The door opened fast and the words came as quickly: "You were to come in!"

He looked at her kneeling on the floor.

"Are you...?" he started to say. And then he shrieked, "You've received." He couldn't avoid the technical term. "You ate it. You...."

His voice was lost in a swirl of action. She backed away from him, fell on the bed, and rolled to the other side. He reached her at the terrace doors and picked her up struggling. Meg's voice reached them screaming, "You don't have to."

But he put her on the ledge and pushed her over.

7

THE PRESENT

Henderson was stretched out on a squeaky frayed sofa in the captain's office; he didn't fit too well; the back of his ankles rested on the arm and his feet dangled slightly; he noticed his shoes needed a shine. He had returned late; it had taken time to get things organized around Lefram: a county coroner had to see him, but he was tied in with a city case; narcotics, highway, homicide divisions were involved, and these ranged from local constables to special investigators; and Lefram was important enough to get a ride back to the city.

"Not many guys use a fully automatic pistol," the captain said. "That takes handling, they go off too easy."

He was a big-framed, thin-looking, bald man with a pleasant voice that might have been selling insurance.

"Probably local too," said Henderson. "There wasn't too much time to get somebody outside. Can't tell though: if they're organized...."

"This guy Keerson. I'd like to hear what he has to say."

"He doesn't have to say anything now."

"Material witness in the girl's death: that'll get him in here. If he's as loony as Lefram thought he was, he might feel like showing us how stupid we are."

"It's an idea," said Henderson. "But he's not careless; it doesn't look as if he's playing to an audience. I'll try him anyway."

The phone rang, and the captain answered.

"Yes, he's here."

Henderson swung off the sofa and took the receiver.

"Yes."

"Am I speaking with Mr. Henderson?"

"Yes, that's right." He looked at the clock: it was ten-fifteen.

"My name is Engelman, David Engelman. I run a shop on Governor Street."

"Yes."

"Here I have a gold locket that a fellow sold me two days ago."

"This is the homicide division, Mr. Engelman, not robbery."

"You think I would ask for you by name, if I didn't want to speak with you."

"Go ahead."

"Like I always do, I tried to get his name, but he wasn't telling me. But I could see he was a cab driver. So I watched him go, and got his number and company. And he turns out to be a Jack Trudel, the fellow that sees the girl commit suicide the other night. So I call you...."

"Well, thanks for the..."

"I'm not finished. This locket is very nice, good work, not seen too often in my line, but funny for a locket. So I check that too. Now what would a cabby be doing with such a locket?"

"Maybe he was going to give it to his girl friend."

"This you don't give to girl friends, Mr. Henderson; it's a pyx. Now I'm no Catholic, but I know...."

"I'll be right over."

He didn't bother ringing. He rode the elevator up to the 11th floor and went directly to number 1125. He depressed the ornamental latch and pushed gently: it wasn't locked. As it swung open he followed it with his gun, walked in quickly and stood just inside, listening. There was nothing to be heard. The only light seemed to be what was coming in through the open door. He waited, to make sure of the perfect silence, and in one move he took a step, touched the door, and closed it as quickly and quietly as he could. Without stopping he changed his position to a crouch on the other side of the door and further into the apartment.

The darkness was complete for a while; and gradually it began to grow into solid shapes so that he could make out a hall, doors, and by shifting his head, a dim patch of ceiling in another room: the spill from a street light

straining its way to the 11th floor. The opening
to that room was too wide for a door; that made
it a living room. He remained motionless for
what felt like a week, and tried to see more of
the vague interior. There was no hurry; Lefram
had said Keerson would know he was coming:
and he might have asked the man with the
impatient gun to come along for a second try.

When nothing seemed to be happening, he
stood upright and inched ahead to see more of
the room where the light filtered in. The floor
creaked under him: it sounded like a cave-in.
He darted as fast as he could manage silently
and felt a wall behind him as he crouched
again. More waiting, more silence, breathing
through his mouth carefully, the light getting
better and better: he decided to try it again.

Somebody grunted and muttered loudly like
a man rudely disturbed in his sleep. Henderson
stiffened with the gun levelled at the living
room. The noise continued. He began to think it
was a set-up for a deadly joke, on him. The
floor was thumped. He brought the gun down
and almost fired as he saw a man face down on
the carpeting with his hands in front of him;
but the hands were empty, just fists that had

struck the floor. He went into the living room and detoured around it till he came to the man. He was still muttering; he was lying near a couch from which he could have slipped earlier. Henderson felt him for a gun and found nothing; he turned him over; nothing glistened and he felt nothing like blood. The man had drooled on the carpeting.

He left him and searched the other rooms slowly, checked the rear entrance, locked the front and went back into the living room where he turned on a table lamp.

The pallor of the man's face made the red splotches stand out. He looked as if his face muscles were squeezing his skull; his cheek-bones glistened and his mouth looked ready to laugh and it didn't move as he muttered. The noise sounded as if it were coming from a drain. Henderson pushed the man into a sitting position and heaved him onto the couch. He propped him upright and shouted at him. It didn't register. He gripped him by the jaw and shook him, still shouting, and the man's eyes opened.

"Can you hear me?"

The eyes looked somewhere into a mist with the universal stare of a camera lens. The muttering had stopped now, a hand moved, then the other; they touched the couch as if he wanted to get up.

"Hey! Can you hear me?"

"Of course." The voice was taut, raspy, just vocal chords making sounds.

"You're Keerson?"

"You don't even know that, do you, Henderson?"

"Routine, friend. Let's pass it."

"Then there won't be much left to talk about. Maybe we could talk about you."

His eyes still weren't looking at anything, and his voice grated out his words like a tired machine. Henderson moved out of line and Keerson didn't follow him.

"The Lucy girl was up in your place three nights ago. She was killed. It seems you were there. That calls for some explaining."

"Yes, it does. Do you think I can explain death, Henderson? Even I can't do that."

"Just *her* death, Keerson, that's all."

"I wish you'd stop calling me Keerson. It's not my name at all."

"Forget it. It's not important."

"Yes, that's so true. It's not important."

"The Lucy girl. Come on."

"Yes? Does she want something?"

Henderson brought the gun up instinctively at the irrationality; and with a sigh he holstered it. He tried to meet the remark with: "Yes, she wants to know how she died."

But all he got back was, "She knows that. Ask her, you'll see."

Henderson was beginning to think this was a job for the police psychiatrists. They could undrug him, or re-drug him, or do whatever it is they do to a gone case.

"They wouldn't do any good," the voice said.

"Who?" asked Henderson quickly, but he had felt the force of the statement. Keerson didn't answer, but something like a laugh came from his throat.

"Talk it up, Keerson. You were having one of your fancy dress balls, and you wound up killing her, didn't you?"

It wasn't the way to question him, but he was trying to get through the mist.

"And what have you got to substantiate that?" Keerson droned on. "A dead madam. And an ex-pimp, also dead." Another laugh followed. "There was no time even for a witnessed statement from him. No time."

"How do you know that?"

"You shouldn't even ask."

"Somebody told you."

"No, of course not."

"Somebody who saw Herby long enough to kill him."

"I haven't seen anybody like that yet."

"All right, how do you know?" asked Henderson quietly: it looked like an opening, he seemed interested.

The man became silent. He didn't move as Henderson asked the question again. He asked a third time, and the muttering began. Keerson started to fidget and finally to speak. He spoke a continual stream of abuse, foul with low metaphor, first angrily, then sniggeringly, his volume rising and his body shaking more and more. Henderson tried to hold him and couldn't. He stepped back and swung his fist squarely at Keerson's forehead like a man punching a horse on a bet. His arm ached right up to the shoulder, and Keerson, who stopped for a moment, seemed to have noticed nothing. Henderson moved back, sweating, his hand touching his gun butt. The muttering returned, and then the raspy speech and the snigger:

187

"You looked at Paula when she was changing to go swimming. You saw it. You didn't really know, it was the first time you had..." And the recital went on into details that puzzled Henderson at first. "...and even though you went to confession,"—a snigger—"you couldn't forget. You really didn't want to. It stayed with you in all its..." And then Henderson remembered: a hot summer, so many years ago, he was a boy, not in high-school yet, no, not then, the girls, the awakening sexuality, his bothersome "sinfulness." The voice skipped years and referred to other things, old resentments against God's justice and doubts still active, but most of it was lost in gibberish, Latin-sounding, and some of it very funny to Keerson, and then a sing-song tone: "You shouldn't be here, you shouldn't be here, Henderson, Henderson, Fenderson, Senderson, Genderson, ha ha ha, gender, sex, Sexerson, ha ha ha. Seven times they drew water from the well, but now they have faucets. Do you have a faucet, Sexerson? Ha ha ha. You've got nothing on me, nothing on me, but I've got lots on you. My name is...." He shrieked, and kept shrieking, as though in pain. Henderson rushed to him and slapped him until he subsided.

"Can you hear me?"

"Of course."

Henderson took out the pyx and held it up.

"What were you doing with this the night she died? Come on, talk!"

Keerson trembled violently and shrieked again. Henderson put the pyx in his pocket and took out a pair of handcuffs. Keerson was on his feet, his face almost tearing open with the strain of his frenzy. His hand flicked out and he snatched the handcuffs from Henderson; he held them up, one bracelet in each hand, like a man holding on to prison bars, and with a mighty knuckle-white gesture, he snapped them in two and approached Henderson with the raised cuffs in his hands. Henderson moved around him and hit him on the head with the barrel of the gun. Keerson slumped, not unconscious, back on the couch. He tried to say something, but his voice dwindled and he shuddered. Finally, he lay still, with his eyes closed.

Henderson sat down in an armchair, very tired, and like a little boy saying his prayers, he made a huge sign of the cross, his gun still in his hand; his terror almost shook him as he remembered that even exorcists often fail.

He didn't know how long he sat there, but

189

eventually he heard Keerson stirring. He watched him with his gun.

Keerson opened his eyes and looked at the ceiling. Slowly, as if he were following a plane in the sky, his head turned until he could see Henderson. He blinked heavily and focussed things a little more.

In a whisper, he said, "Who are you?"

Henderson looked at him for what seemed a long time, and answered, "Police. You'll have to come with me."

Keerson turned away and muttered, "You saw me...?"

"Yes."

"Why didn't you shoot me then? It would have been all over."

Henderson didn't answer.

"Why didn't you,...then...?" Keerson tried to sit up, but he rolled off the couch onto the floor and drew himself to his hands and knees. When he saw the broken handcuffs, he reached for one of the bracelets and knelt there with it. Henderson was out of his chair, still watching with the gun.

"Do it now, whoever you are, finish it off, now. Do it before....I don't control it any more.

After I...after she...died, it came over me fully, at last, with....I thought I had the power to...it felt as if I was ruling. But it's beyond me now, it's everywhere in me, I can't command...the chaos."

He shuddered as he spoke. He wasn't addressing Henderson now but something present in his own unchanging eyes. Henderson looked around for a telephone and didn't see one; as he began edging toward the hall, Keerson's words held him.

"...it won't be ruled any more....It's stronger. I thought I was....Is there any way to rule you?" His voice rose as he hissed the words in an agony of frustration. "I've done...everything. I've sacrificed...but she...she was the one who was stronger. She...finish me off, you, with the gun, do it, will you? Do it."

Henderson said quietly, "I can't. Let's go before things get worse."

"Can't!" he whined painfully. "It's easy. You've got the power, there, in the gun."

"You can't die this way."

"It's so easy...die this way?" Keerson's body went rigid for a moment. He turned toward Henderson and stood up swiftly.

"Die? I can't die. I'm immortal. You're afraid
to have me die this way? Do it! Whoever you
are, do it! Hurry...." His voice became thick
then and his eyes looked at nothing. His next
word was, "Henderson!"

Henderson grew cold when he heard his
name again.

"...you're afraid to see me die, Henderson.
You're afraid you'll...damn me, ha, ha. You're a
believer, Henderson, one of the good, and you
think you'll be damning me..."

"Keerson!" Henderson shouted, but it had
no effect.

"...you and your petty goodness! You...." He
shrieked at Henderson and abused him so violently his words were unintelligible "...sending
me to hell, ha, ha, ha. You'll be sinning, Henderson, you'll be responsible for my soul. You're in
full control of it, you'll be like me, me! You'll be
like God..." He shrieked again and hurled out
Latin words as if he were tearing real objects to
pieces. "...destroy your petty goodness. Would
you kill me, and still believe?" He laughed at
that. "Would you rather die than...sin?" He
sniggered at the word until he was laughing in
bellows.

Henderson shouted at him again, but there was no getting through to him now.

"...from you, from you, from you, I'll take your gun, easily, you know, easily..."

Henderson backed away and stood behind the armchair. Keerson, still yelling in broken phrases, took the chair and threw it aside.

"Keerson!" Henderson's hands were so wet he could hardly hold the gun straight. He yelled at Keerson again and fired a shot into the ceiling. Keerson didn't notice it. Henderson kept backing away; he tripped over something he didn't see and fell to the floor against the wall. Keerson's hands darted out and caught nothing, but he tugged at the imagined object and tore open his own hands. He moved to Henderson.

The gun was slippery. Henderson held it in both hands and rested it on his knee. Carefully, he cocked it, and was going to wait, but as he aimed it, Keerson advanced screaming, and he shot him in the head.

When Henderson reached him finally, Keerson's mouth was forming words that he never spoke, and his eyes had a look, perhaps of gratitude, that seemed to come from the depths of his personality. Henderson knelt beside him, trembling; and as his tension subsided, he realized he had been weeping.

He was back in the captain's office, alone. He didn't feel like God, he only felt old. From the squeaky sofa he looked at the dirty ceiling and imagined it to be a sheet of paper, the page on which he'd be writing a report; it needed washing, somebody'll write out a memo. When the others had arrived at Keerson's apartment, he gave them the essential facts and left. He had stopped for a drink someplace and driven carefully back to headquarters. The essential facts. He thought of the official phrases: resisting arrest, assaulting an officer, performance of duty, self-defence. Keep it that way, it's a lot simpler. Why complicate it? Why say...? What could you say? Even about her? Elizabeth Lucy, née Denis, died in a fall after having...was presumably the victim of a homicide resulting from...surmisable but unknown circumstances. The official word. Henderson re-examined the ceiling and thought of the report: now, while it's still fresh; memory can play tricks; get it down on paper, as it happened, just the facts, no interpretations. What's a fact without an interpretation?

Reluctantly, he got up and went into another room to the desk he always used. He looked in the drawer for paper, threw out the rose he had taken in the morgue, and put a sheet in the old typewriter in front of him. Just as he had the first few sentences organized, a young detective came in.

"Guy here to see you, Lieutenant."

"Who is he?"

"A Colonel Denis. He said you were expecting him."

"Oh, yeah. I've got to take him to the morgue."

"Shall I send him in?"

"No. I'll be right out."

The door closed. Henderson took the paper out of the typewriter and put it back in the drawer. He grimaced with irony as he thought that the news he had to tell the Colonel was, after all, good.